One minute, they were just friends.

The next minute, Will's mouth was on hers. And before Lisa could think, she was drawn into a kiss that deepened and grew. Forgotten was the comfort she had intended to give him, to help him get over the pain. What remained was passion.

At long last, they drew apart in stunned surprise.

Then Will smiled. "I think I've been wondering how that would feel for a long, long time."

"How did it feel, Lieutenant?" she asked, shaken by the strength of his kiss.

He threaded his hand through her hair. "I think I need more evidence," he murmured.

So they kissed again. With a hunger devouring in its intensity. Until that moment, Lisa hadn't realized she was starving for this man's touch....

Dear Reader,

Welcome to Silhouette **Special Edition** . . . welcome to romance. Each month, Silhouette **Special Edition** publishes six novels with you in mind—stories of love and life, tales that you can identify with—romance with that little "something special" added in.

This month, we're pleased to present the conclusion of Nora Roberts's enchanting new series, THE DONOVAN LEGACY. *Charmed* is the story of Boone Sawyer and Anastasia Donovan—and their magical, charmed love. Don't miss this wonderful tale!

Sherryl Woods's warm, tender series—VOWS—will light up this Thanksgiving month. *Honor*—Kevin and Lacey Halloran's story—will be followed next month by *Cherish*. The vows that three generations of Halloran men live by create timeless tales that you'll want to keep forever!

Rounding out the November lineup are books from other favorite writers: Arlene James, Celeste Hamilton, Victoria Pade and Kim Cates. This is truly a feast for romance readers this month!

I hope that you enjoy this book and all the stories to come. Happy Thanksgiving Day—and all of us at Silhouette Books wish you the most wonderful holiday season ever!

Sincerely,

Tara Gavin
Senior Editor
Silhouette Books

CELESTE HAMILTON

FATHER FIGURE

Silhouette®

SPECIAL EDITION®

Published by Silhouette Books New York

America's Publisher of Contemporary Romance

For Leigh Neely, who always talks me through it.

SILHOUETTE BOOKS
300 East 42nd St., New York, N.Y. 10017

FATHER FIGURE

ISBN: 0-373-09779-4

First Silhouette Books printing November 1992

All the characters in this book have no existence outside the imagination of the author and have no relation whatsoever to anyone bearing the same name or names. They are not even distantly inspired by any individual known or unknown to the author, and all incidents are pure invention.

®: Trademark used under license and registered in the United States Patent and Trademark Office and in other countries.

Printed in the U.S.A.

CELESTE HAMILTON

has been writing since she was ten years old, with the encouragement of parents who told her she could do anything she set out to do and teachers who helped her refine her talents.

The broadcast media captured her interest in high school, and she graduated from the University of Tennessee with a B.S. in Communications. From there, she began writing and producing commercials at a Chattanooga, Tennessee, radio station.

Celeste began writing romances in 1985 and now works at her craft full-time. Married to a policeman, she likes nothing better than spending time at home with him and their two much-loved cats, although she and her husband also enjoy traveling when their busy schedules permit. Wherever they go, however, "It's always nice to come home to East Tennessee—one of the most beautiful corners of the world."

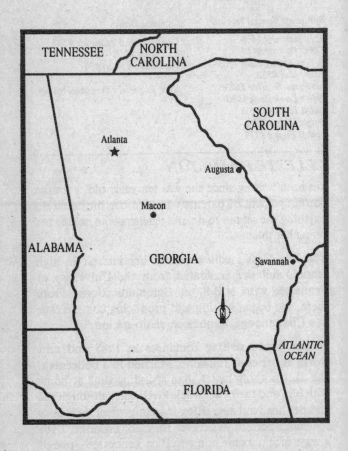

Prologue

The gun barrel was cold. Icy, like the November wind. But not half as frozen as the eyes of the man who pressed the revolver into Lisa's cheek.

"I might as well kill you now," he whispered. No regret blurred his flat emotionless tones.

Lisa forced herself to speak slowly. "Killing me will only make things worse."

His laughter was loud, out of control. "It can't get any worse. You made sure of that. And you're going to pay."

She knew better than to struggle. This man had already murdered once tonight. He was one pull of the trigger away from doing it again. *Think,* she told herself. *You're a cop. Sixteen years a cop. So think, damn it, think of a maneuver to get out of this.*

But this man, himself twenty-seven years an Atlanta cop, had left her no room for maneuvers. She was pinned at the corner of a rooftop parking lot, her back against a low concrete barrier. Behind her was a certain death drop down the side of the building. Stairs were to their left. His gun was to her right. Her options were limited enough to make her abductor gloat.

His voice blended with the shriek of the wind. "Guess you're caught this time, Talbot. Guess you won't be putting that pretty nose in—"

The *ping* of the elevator cut him short. Because he was surprised, Lisa was able to twist away and call out a warning. "He's got a gun." But she wasn't quick enough to save herself. She expected the gun to fire as her abductor once more pulled her tight to him. She expected to die. She didn't expect to hear Will call her name.

Will Espinoza. Her partner. Her lover.

Will. Her captor's nephew. The man who loved him like a son loves a father.

Will stepped from the shadows near the elevator, hands outstretched, the parking lot lights glinting off his black, deadly automatic. "Let her go, Mickey," he said, his voice breaking on the other man's name.

They were so alike, these two men. The imprint of their Cuban and Anglo ancestries was mixed in their regular, handsome features. Both were intelligent and strong, ruthless in pursuit of a goal. And Lisa was trapped between them.

"Let her go," Will repeated as he walked forward.

Mickey Vallejo's gun twisted against Lisa's cheekbone again. "I can't do it." She felt the muscles tighten in his chest. "I can't let her go. Not even for you, Will."

Will moved closer, his eyes never wavering from his uncle. "I can help you, Mickey. But you have to let Lisa go."

"Yeah," Mickey whispered, and for the first time his voice held some life, some hope. "Yeah, you can help me. We can set this up to look like an accident. We've worked enough murders to know—"

"One last dirty deed from a dirty cop, huh?" Will cut in.

Lisa knew, if she lived, she would never forget the anguished, accusatory sound of his voice.

For several long moments the two men stared at each other.

Mickey broke the silence. "So you know all about it, do you, Will? You're prepared to sit in judgment on me? You, who I raised. You, who I trained—"

"You didn't train me to kill innocent people."

"I taught you to care about family."

"No," Will said. "You taught me to be honorable. You said a man without honor has nothing." For just a moment, his dark gaze intercepted Lisa's. She could see how he struggled to remain calm. The sane, reasonable cop was at war with his personal feelings. His gaze flickered back to Mickey. "Live by your words, Uncle. Let her go."

Though his grip on her hadn't loosened, Lisa could feel the trembling that had started in Mickey. "She knows too much," he muttered.

Police sirens sounded in the distance.

"Everyone knows," Will whispered.

Mickey pulled Lisa toward the stairs. "I can still get away. You'll give me some time, won't you, Will? I'll take Lisa—"

"No!" Will said, following them. "Stop it, Mickey. You're caught. Don't make it worse. Let her go. Take me if you want a hostage. Just let her go."

But Lisa knew any chance of reasoning with Mickey was gone. At the top of the stairs he stopped, and once more the muzzle of the gun dug into her cheek.

"Choose," Mickey shouted at Will, hysteria in his voice. "It's me or her. Your choice, Will."

He must have found an answer in his nephew's face.

Against Lisa's ear, he murmured something in Spanish.

Then Will's anguished cry mixed with the gun's report.

Chapter One

Heavy wooden doors swung shut behind Will Espinoza as he stepped into an empty corridor. The sunshine streaming through the window in front of him was a surprise. It seemed only a moment ago he had been on a dark rooftop, with the cold wind in his face, with Lisa and Mickey and the sound of a gun—

Voices at the far end of the hall interrupted his troubling thoughts, and he looked around for an escape. Though here at police headquarters it would be difficult to hide, he just couldn't deal with any more questions or curious glances or expressions of sympathy. Hoping he hadn't been spotted, he stepped into an alcove formed by the deep-set windows.

The group of officers went down the hall without noticing him. Relieved, Will leaned a shoulder against the wall and gazed out the window. He wanted a cigarette—bad. For five years he had lived happily without nicotine. Now the craving was a daily occurrence.

A week had passed since that awful night with Mickey and Lisa, a week in which every day had been spent in trying not to remember. Today however, he had been forced to recall every detail for an Internal Affairs investigatory panel. He had relived it all—moment by horrible moment. He had once more been confronted by Mickey's betrayal.

"Damn him," Will whispered. He felt tired and old, much older than thirty-four, much wiser than he had been this time last week.

How he wished he were without such bitter wisdom.

More voices sounded in the hall, and a couple of guys stopped at the water fountain just beyond the alcove. Will didn't move, hoping they would pass just as the others had. Then one of the men mentioned his name, and he strained forward to hear.

"You're right," a second man replied, his words easily audible. "Espinoza had to know something. He and Mickey were tight. He must have been in on the take."

Heat rushed to Will's face, but he remained motionless.

"They say Mickey had a finger in a lot of pies," the first speaker said. "He's been on the take for years and years. Everyone's walking around saying they can't believe it, that he always seemed true blue. But I always did think there was something funny about him."

"What's funny is how his *loyal* nephew ended up assigned to an Internal Affairs corruption probe."

They laughed knowingly; Will's hands doubled into fists.

The second speaker continued, "Espinoza didn't do Mickey any good, though. He forgot to clue his pretty little partner in on his uncle's side businesses. She was going to turn Mickey in. Then he freaked out."

"Now *I* can think of a few clues for a partner who looks like Lisa Talbot...."

This time the men's laughter pushed Will's fury over the edge. Hands clenched at his sides, he stepped from the alcove. "Have you two got something you want to say to me?"

The officers spun around to face him, their mouths gaping in surprise. The younger officer Will didn't recognize. He couldn't even meet Will's gaze. The older man, who had made the comment about Lisa, was a florid-faced detective named Ken Robbins. He stepped forward, a weak smile on his lips. "Espinoza, we...uh...we didn't know you were here."

"Of course not," Will retorted, moving closer. "You wouldn't have the guts to say any of that to my face."

Though Robbins flushed a deeper shade of crimson, he backed off, holding up his hand. "Listen, I'm sorry. We were just talking, you know. What happened to Mickey...it's got us all rattled. But I apologize. I know this is a bad time for you—"

"And how the hell do you know that?" Will demanded, his agitation fueled by the man's bumbling attempt at sympathy. Pity was the last thing he wanted from anyone.

The man tried again. "What I know is that our jobs are tough enough without—"

Will cut him off with a derisive expletive. "When was the last time you did anything tough? You've always seemed pretty comfortable at your safe little desk."

Anger replaced Robbins' conciliatory expression. He shook off his friend's detaining hand and looked Will straight in the eye. "The way I hear it, pretty soon you won't have a desk around here."

"Maybe you ought to stop believing the department gossip and start concentrating on your own job."

Robbins came closer, until his leering face was just inches from Will's. "I don't think it's gossip, Espinoza. A person can smell a dirty cop, and right now, you stink about as bad as your uncle."

Fury burned the last bit of caution from Will's brain. Before he could act, however, his arm was caught from behind and a familiar voice muttered, "Let's just end this right here, why don't we?"

Jerking away, Will wheeled around and met Lieutenant Andy Baskin's steady gaze. Andy had once been Will's partner, and was his boss on the Internal Affairs investigation in which Mickey had been caught. In the years they had worked together, Will had learned to read Andy's expressions, and right now the warning in his blue eyes checked Will's vehement protest. It was a good thing, too. For standing just behind Andy, in the open door of the conference room, were the members of the Internal Affairs panel who had questioned Will so thoroughly. And all five of them—four men and a woman—were frowning.

Andy cuffed him lightly on the shoulder. "Weren't we going for a cup of coffee?"

Will glanced from Andy to the panel and then back to Robbins. Much as he wanted to rearrange the detective's smirking features, this wasn't the right time. He nodded at Andy.

A murmur ran through the I.A. panel as they dispersed.

With a gesture that was half pat on the back and half shove, Andy started Will forward. Andy paused only once, in front of the still-glowering Robbins, where he murmured, "Nice jacket you're wearing there, Ken. If you watch your mouth in the future, nobody'll be tempted to put any wrinkles in it."

This time when the older man protested, his friend pulled him away.

Midway down the hall, Will muttered, "I can fight my own battles, Baskin."

Andy chuckled. "Indulge me, okay? I have this complex about seeing a friend ruin his career."

"A pencil pusher like Ken Robbins couldn't ruin anything for me."

"I know the man is a gossip and a busybody, but punching him out in the hall wouldn't earn you any medals. Especially considering the audience back there."

As they turned the corner, Will drew up short. "What did they ask you after I finished making my statement?"

Thrusting a hand through his tawny hair, Andy looked away. "We'll talk about them some other time." He glanced over his shoulder and quickly changed the subject. "How's Elena?"

Thoughts of his grieving Aunt Elena wiped every other consideration from Will's mind. In the ways that mattered, Elena and Mickey had been his parents. Elena was a semi-invalid who suffered from the debilitating effects of rheumatoid arthritis. Will had always been protective of her. Telling her what Mickey had done was one of the worst moments of his life.

"Elena's surviving," Will told Andy. "But I don't think all the consequences have occurred to her yet."

"Underneath that fragile exterior, she's a tough lady. But she's got plenty to worry about without your getting in trouble around here. That should be incentive enough for you to keep your nose clean."

Will couldn't argue with his friend's logic. Usually a loudmouth like Robbins wouldn't bother him, but everything was so screwed up these days. He was reeling from it all—Mickey's betrayal. Elena's devastation. He wondered if he would ever move past these tragedies.

"Hello, Will."

The voice was unmistakable, and it brought Will face-to-face with his other tragedy. "Lisa," he murmured as she walked toward him.

She was alive. Every once in a while, Will had to remind himself that Mickey hadn't shot her. She was here, her shoulders straight in a subdued gray jacket, her hair pulled back from her face, her blue eyes nearly black with concern. Will's gaze locked for a moment with hers. She waited expectantly, but he said nothing before he looked away. Shoving his hands into his pockets, he stared down the hall as Andy and Lisa exchanged greetings.

Until last week, looking at Lisa had been one of the chief pleasures of Will's life. Hell, there wasn't a man alive who couldn't appreciate Lisa. She had a glow about her that went deeper than her creamy skin and blue eyes. She wasn't a classic beauty; her appeal was more wholesome than that. Long and lean, rounded in all the right places, she was the typical American male's fantasy. Yet there was something in her smile that reminded Will of the tomboy who had lived next door when he was a kid. Lisa was a physical woman, athletic, and it showed in the way she moved. Catlike. Graceful. Just watching her walk across the room had often stirred him to erectness.

But as she moved toward him now, all he could think of was the way Mickey's gun had pressed to her head. He could see her pale, drawn features and her moonbeam-blond hair blowing in the wind. He could hear the gutsy warning she had called out to him. He could feel the terror and remorse that gripped him when he had pulled his gun on Mickey. What had gone through Mickey's mind in that moment after he'd asked Will to choose between himself and Lisa? Will would never know.

For Mickey was dead.

"Will," Lisa said again.

He forced himself to look at her.

She pressed on, "Was the panel rough this morning?"

He shrugged. "I didn't tell them anything that isn't in our reports. I'm not even sure why they insisted on talking to me."

"You had to know they'd be calling you in," Andy said. "Given the circumstances—"

"The circumstances?" Will interrupted, frowning. "The circumstances are that Mickey betrayed his badge, Lisa caught him, then he went berserk, tried to kill her and blew his own head off. What's so complicated about that?"

Lisa made a soft sound of protest.

"This isn't the place for this conversation," Andy said as he urged them both toward an exit. Nothing more was said until they reached the parking lot beside the building.

Squinting in the unseasonably warm November sunshine, Will faced his two friends again. "I'm sorry, I know you both are trying to help, but—"

"But you don't want our help," Andy completed for him. "What you would like to do is go crawl into a hole somewhere." He shook his head. "We can't let you do that."

Andy's tone was matter-of-fact rather than pitying, but Will glared at him just the same.

A hint of steel crept into Lisa's soft voice. "Sooner or later you're going to have to talk about it, Will."

"I talked about it all morning."

"Not to them. To me."

He took a deep breath and closed his eyes, but when he opened them, Lisa was still waiting. He knew her, knew she wouldn't give up until they examined what had happened with Mickey from every possible angle. Her ability and desire to get at the heart of the matter was one quality that made her a great cop. Will had always admired her determination. And in some strange, inexplicable way, her directness was what had turned him on from the moment they met.

But that was before. Now all Will wanted was some distance from everything and everyone who reminded him of how far Mickey had fallen from honor.

Lisa was alive. For that much, Will would always be grateful. But she had come close to death. And for that, he knew he would always feel responsible. He should have known that something wasn't right with his uncle. The signs were all there.

Damn it, why hadn't he known?

Like a jackhammer, the question pounded in his head. "I've gotta go," he mumbled, turning on his heel. He just couldn't stand here with Lisa any longer.

"Terry's been asking for you," she said.

The words made him turn back. Terry was Lisa's son, a nearly ten-year-old bundle of energy and curiosity, a bright boy who loved his mother but was hungry for male attention and companionship. Will could identify with those feelings; he had been in the same situation at Terry's age. In the last couple of years, he and Terry had become good friends. Since Will's relationship with Lisa had changed and deepened, his interest in Terry had changed, also. But he hadn't even spoken to the boy in the past week.

Lisa continued. "The news about Mickey has been hard on him, Will."

It would be, Will thought. Lisa and Terry had become part of his family, and that included Mickey and Elena. "What did you tell Terry?" he asked her.

"As much of the truth as I thought he could understand."

"Terry's smart," Andy put in. "But death's a hard concept to grasp at that age."

The flicker of sadness on his friend's face reminded Will that Andy had lost a brother when he was only twelve. The tragedy had propelled Andy into police work, but he had told Will that his family never sat down to talk about his brother's death, leaving scars Andy had only dealt with in recent years. Will's own father had died when he was younger than Terry, so he knew the kinds of questions and fears a kid could have at a time like this. As much as Will wanted to run away, as much as he detested even speaking Mickey's name, Terry deserved a chance to talk this over with him. It was the only decent thing to do.

He looked at Lisa again. "I'll come see him tonight. Is seven okay?"

Lisa agreed and started to ask him for dinner, but he didn't give her a chance. Without once glancing at her or Andy again, he just walked away. The hollowness in the pit of her stomach spread to her chest, where it changed to an ache. What she wanted was to run after Will, put her arms around him and tell him it would all be okay. But he could barely look at her. She could only imagine what would happen if she tried to touch him.

"Damn," Andy muttered. "He's like a zombie."

"It's only been a week," Lisa said, trying to be optimistic. "We have to give him some time. He hasn't had time to grieve."

"That's the problem. He's so angry right now that he can't grieve. He won't allow himself to miss Mickey, to feel sorry that he's dead. He feels betrayed, and he's furious."

"It isn't easy to see your hero topple."

Running a hand along his clean-shaven jaw, Andy frowned at Will's fast-retreating figure. "Mickey was a hero to a lot of people around here. He's got a list of commendations a mile long, and he was always ready to help out a fellow officer. He listened to everyone's problems."

Lisa swung her purse strap over her shoulder. "Like I put in my report, that fatherly concern seemed to be part of Mickey's strategy. He knew everyone's secrets—who was having financial trouble, who was unhappy about their latest assignment. My informant said Mickey knew who was ripe for corruption. He would pass those names on to pimps, dealers and bookies— anyone who could benefit from having a cop in their pocket. In payment, they cut Mickey into their action."

"Where did the money go, do you think?"

"From what I was told, he gambled a lot. And of course, he used a lot of it for Elena. She has a full-time nurse and a housekeeper. He built her a greenhouse and a pool." She sighed sadly. "Mickey always told everyone that the money came from an inheritance he had invested years ago. He was such a great guy that no one thought of questioning how he afforded his lifestyle."

"I suppose Mickey thought the end justified the means," Andy murmured. "He probably told himself he was doing it all for Elena's sake."

Having been witness to the tenderness with which Mickey had treated his wife, Lisa couldn't believe otherwise. "He was devoted to her," she insisted. "I'm sure of that."

Andy shook his head. "Yeah, he loved her so much that he led a double life."

"It's difficult to reconcile all I know about him now with the man who used to spend Sunday afternoons tossing a football to my son."

Two images clicked through her head—Mickey and Will romping with Terry in the bright October sunshine and then Mickey's face, mottled with rage as he threatened to kill her. The juxtaposition was dizzying enough for Lisa to sway on her feet.

"Hey, there," Andy said as he grabbed her arm to steady her. "Are you sure you're doing okay?"

She took a deep breath. "I'm fine."

But Andy didn't appear to believe her. "I don't think you should go before that panel right now."

"Don't be silly. There's no reason for me not to answer a few questions."

"Everyone would understand. You've been through hell."

"So has Will, and he showed up today."

"And he came out of there ready to take a swing at the first person who looked at him." Tersely, Andy told her about Will's encounter with Ken Robbins.

Lisa groaned. "God, what if he had decked him?"

"I imagine he'll tear into someone before all this is over. If the circumstances had been different, I'd say that weasel Robbins would be a pretty good choice."

"The talk will die down soon."

Andy grunted. "Don't count on it."

Lisa looked at him in surprise. "What do you mean?"

"Oh, come on, Lisa, think about it. Will is Mickey's nephew. Just like Robbins, there are plenty of people who are going to assume that Will's been in on this." He cocked his head to the side, watching her closely as he added, "They'll think the same about us."

She stared at him, shocked.

"Guilty by association," Andy said.

"But Will wasn't in on it. And we weren't, either."

Andy shrugged.

Lisa grabbed his arm. "Damn, Andy, you don't suspect Will and me of something, do you?"

His denial was vehement. "Good God, no! I would trust you and Will with my life. You're both the best. I handpicked you to be on this I.A. team with me because of how much I trust you."

"Then what is the problem?"

"Not everyone knows us, Lisa. And even you have to admit it looks pretty damn suspicious that we were conducting an investigation that led straight to Mickey."

Lisa still didn't understand. "Why would I have been ready to take Mickey in if I were in on some scheme or cover-up with him?"

"Maybe not everyone thinks what happened that night went down exactly the way we're saying it did. After all, we were the first three officers on the scene."

Lisa's heart pounded in rhythm with the fury that pumped through her. Not once in her entire career had she been accused of bending the truth. Now she understood why Will had been tempted to take a swing at Ken Robbins. "It's crazy," she fumed. "What do they think happened?"

"I've been told some people are saying it was a lover's triangle—Mickey and Will fighting over you."

Lisa felt as if her head would explode. "All of this is absurd."

"I agree," Andy said. "But it is common knowledge that you and Will are more than just friends. And you know how some people feel about partners becoming involved."

"But where did the suspicions about Mickey and me come from?"

"Who knows where people think up this stuff." Andy bit his lip, seeming to hesitate, then plunged ahead. "The other story is worse. They're saying Mickey's suicide was really murder."

The world melted before Lisa's eyes. Cars, buildings, sky—all the colors ran together, blurred. It was as if all that she knew, the principles she held dearest—honor, decency, truth—were turning upsidedown.

The truth about that night was that she had gone to meet a possible informant, a woman who had identified Mickey as the inside man at the police department. Lisa had wanted to be convinced of the woman's story before she involved Will. She had just called Will and Andy and asked them to meet her at the apartment when Mickey showed up. He shot the woman and dragged Lisa up to the rooftop parking garage. When Will and Andy found the informant dead, they called for backup and fanned out over the building in a frantic search for Lisa. Thus, the rooftop confrontation.

It amazed Lisa that the tragic, but true, facts had been twisted into something even more vile. If these rumors hurt her this much, she could only imagine how they would tear Will apart inside. And he had been through enough.

Angry enough to take on the world, she turned back toward headquarters. "I'm going to stop all this right now," she said through clenched teeth. "I'm not going to see Will hurt any more. There's not one shred of evidence to support any of these ridiculous stories. I'm going to make sure—"

Andy caught her elbow, forcing her to stop. "Just hold it a minute, will you. For what my opinion's worth, I don't believe the powers that be really think you or I or Will were involved with Mickey's dirty dealings at all. But there are rumors and gossip floating through every precinct in the city."

"If they're listening to squad-room talk—"

"I didn't say they were believing all these stories. But they've got to check out some possibilities. If what your informant said was true—"

"*If* it's true?" Lisa sputtered. "Mickey admitted everything to me up on that roof."

"All right, so we know Mickey was on the take. Now the focus of the investigation turns to those people he drew into his scams with him. Every bozo cop who ever looked the other way from a street corner drug deal has to be shaking in his or her shoes right now. I.A. is looking to clean house."

"Good. I have a few ideas about who might have something to hide. I'm going to rattle—"

"You won't be rattling anything," Andy said. "You're off the investigation. You, me and Will are being reassigned."

Lisa put a hand to her forehead, feeling stupid. Of course they were off the case. How could any of them conduct an investigation when they were the suspects?

"God, Andy," she whispered. "I'm so sorry. You've wanted this I.A. assignment for a long time."

"I'll be back," he said with his customary confidence. "I've got nothing to hide. Neither do you. Or Will. We've all just got to sit tight until this is over."

Sit tight. That wouldn't be easy while co-workers whispered behind their backs, when they were forced into defending their past actions. But Lisa knew Andy was right. There was nothing else any of them could do. She thought she could handle it. As for Will . . . well, that was another story.

"I don't know how he'll make it through this."

Andy didn't need to ask to whom she referred. "Will's going to need you, Lisa."

She thought of the suffering but stoic man who had stalked away from her earlier. "He won't admit to needing me right now."

"That'll pass."

"I'm glad you're so sure of it. I'm not."

"Hey, I never thought the two of you would end up together in the first place, and you proved me wrong."

"We're not together right now."

"It's temporary. Meg said you two were fated for romance from the start."

Lisa scoffed, "Your wife, the soothsayer."

"Well, she was right," Andy pointed out, grinning. "In the beginning it looked to me as if all you and Will were going to do was argue. Then you became friends." His grin grew broader. "And more."

More. That simple word didn't begin to describe the depth of passion Lisa had found in Will's arms, the sense of completeness that had grown from their ever-deepening friendship. She was thirty-seven years old, and the disappointments in her life had long ago taught her that romantic love was a fairy tale. But she and Will had begun something together. Neither of them trusted easily, but each had started to let the other inside. With Will, Lisa hadn't felt the need for barriers. He had been the same with her. Until now. Now everything had changed. His emotional barriers had been reinforced.

Would he ever let her close again?

"You need to go in," Andy said, holding his watch up for her to see.

Mentally composing herself, Lisa nodded. "I hope I can hold my temper."

He took her hand and squeezed it. "You can do it."

She managed a smile and started to walk away, but Andy held her back.

"There's one more thing," he said, and his grin disappeared. "Watch yourself."

She didn't understand what he meant. "I'm just going to tell the truth."

"I don't mean in front of the panel. Like I said before, everyone who ever did anything wrong is going to be on edge for a while. Some people might think you know more than you do."

Lisa began to follow his logic. "They might think Mickey told me some names, you mean."

"Exactly. So be careful. People could get a little crazy. Probably not, but you never know."

"Okay, Hotshot," Lisa said, using the nickname she had bestowed on Andy in his gung-ho rookie days. "Don't worry about me. I can take care of myself."

Andy pulled her to him for a brief, hard hug, a gesture that bespoke the deep affection between them. "Nobody stands a chance against you."

Squaring her shoulders, Lisa crossed the parking lot and went inside to face the I.A. panel.

Hours later, as she sat at her own kitchen table, she understood why Will had looked like the walking dead after his own session with those five officers.

Cupping her warm coffee mug between both hands, Lisa closed her eyes and tried to let the familiar, everyday sounds of her home calm her. The refrigerator gurgled as ice dropped into a bin in the freezer. The clock radio on the kitchen counter hummed. And from the living room came the muted laughter of Terry, who was playing one of his favorite video games.

It was all so normal, so far from that night of terror with Mickey, a giant leap from the pointed questions she had answered this afternoon. The I.A. panel hadn't wasted any time in targeting the key issues. Their voices still rang in Lisa's ears.

"Did you have knowledge of Captain Miguel Vallejo's illegal activities before you began the Internal Affairs investigation?"

"Did Lieutenant Espinoza at any time discuss his uncle's corrupt activities with you?"

"What about Lieutenant Baskin?"

"Tell us again how you came to suspect Captain Vallejo."

"Tell us, if you will, just what is the exact nature of your relationship with Lieutenant Espinoza?"

"When you went to the informant's apartment, why didn't you take your partner, Lieutenant Espinoza, with you?"

"Since you were trying to protect Lieutenant Espinoza's feelings that night, would you now lie to protect him?"

That last question had burned like a firebrand. She still couldn't quite believe what they had been implying. Andy might think those questions were just routine, that the panel didn't really believe the ugly rumors, but Lisa wasn't sure.

The only thing she knew for certain was that she had told the truth. It hadn't been easy to admit she and Will were lovers. She wasn't ashamed of their relationship, but Andy was right. Romantic involvement between officers, while not forbidden, was frowned upon. And Lisa couldn't help but believe her relationship with Will could somehow be used against all of them. After all, that ridiculous story about a lover's triangle had started somewhere. Perhaps even with Mickey. She knew he had been insane the night he killed himself. When had he snapped? What sort of stories had he been capable of spreading? And to what end? After all Andy had told her this afternoon, Lisa would believe just about anything.

Telling herself to calm down, she took a sip of coffee. It was lukewarm and bitter. She got up to dump it into the sink, but her hands were shaking so that she dropped the mug to the floor, where it shattered.

"Damn!" she said, disgusted by her weakness.

From the kitchen doorway, Terry chastised her. "Mom, you always tell me not to say that."

She forced herself to smile as she turned to face him. "I guess you caught me, son. I promise it won't happen again."

Terry's blue eyes were solemn as he regarded her. Though everyone told Lisa that he resembled her, there were times, like now, that she thought him the image of his father. Rich Talbot had always looked at her in this same manner when she did anything that was the slightest bit out of character. Eight years ago, in another kitchen, when she had announced she was leaving him, Rich had cocked his head and stared at her just as Terry was doing now.

"Is something wrong?" her son asked, much as his father might have done.

Those who don't believe in the relationship of genes to behavior should study my son, Lisa thought. As she stooped to pick up the pieces of the broken mug, she said, "There's nothing wrong. Go back to your game."

"I thought you said Will was coming tonight."

Lisa bit her lip and glanced at the clock. Will was late. She shouldn't have told Terry that he was coming. He might not show. But she would deal with that if it happened. "You'll know when Will gets here." She straightened and dumped the broken mug in the trash. "Go do your homework."

"I did it already. You even looked at it. Don't you remember?"

She didn't remember, but that didn't mean anything. When she had arrived home this afternoon, she had been too addled by her session at headquarters to do much more than go through the motions of their evening routine.

"Mom—"

"Terry, go back in the living room," she said, her voice sharper than was necessary.

He folded his arms across his chest and glared at her. "Golly, what did I do, anyway?"

She took a deep breath. "I'm sorry. I've just got a lot on my mind."

"About Uncle Mickey?"

The "uncle" made her pause. She had forgotten that Terry had adopted Will's way of addressing Mickey. God, what a nightmare all this was.

"Mom?" Terry prompted.

She looked up. "What?"

"Are you sick or something?"

The worried look on his gamin face would melt a heart much harder than his mother's. He was far too perceptive for his years, far too protective of her, and she loved him for both those qualities. Smiling, she held out her arms. "Come here, little worrywart."

He crossed the room and hugged her. Almost two years ago, when he had turned eight, he had decided hugs were for sissies, and these cuddly moments had become rare. So Lisa made the most of her opportunity, holding him until he squirmed and protested, "Gee, Mom, do you have to?"

She released him, but couldn't resist planting a kiss on the top of his silky blond hair. "Nothing is the matter with me," she told him. "Now go back to your silly game."

He raced from the kitchen, his worries seemingly forgotten. But as Lisa cleaned spilled coffee from the floor, she wondered what was really going on in her son's head. Three years ago she had been shot in the line of duty and had almost died. Terry had begged her to stop being a cop then, and she had very nearly granted him his wish.

Will had helped her remember that police work wasn't just a job to her. What she did and the fervor with which she did it, were part of who she was. He had made her see that leaving the force would be a betrayal of herself. She had stuck with the job.

Terry had no choice but to accept her decision. But at six years old, how could he have expressed what he really felt? How did he feel about her job now? When asked, he said he was proud of her. But there were times when she wasn't sure. Was staying in a sometimes dangerous job fair to her son?

Unbidden, Andy's words of warning flashed through her head. Anxious to get her statement to the panel out of the way, she had brushed his concerns aside. He was being overcautious. If she had the names of anyone who had been involved with Mickey, she would have already given them to I.A. Surely no one would be stupid enough to harass her about it now. There was no reason to worry about that.

Was there?

Once more, Lisa listened to the sounds of her home, willing them to soothe her. But it didn't work. Outside her snug little house, the night was calm. But all she could hear was a howling wind. All she could feel was the cold, black metal of Mickey's gun pressing into her cheek.

"No," she said aloud, struggling to get hold of her emotions. She wasn't going through this again. She had experienced the same sort of panic attacks three years ago after the shooting. Flashbacks, paranoia, rapid pulse rate, fear—all part of posttraumatic stress, the staff shrink had said. All normal reactions. She should take deep breaths and focus on something else until the moment passed.

Will had helped her through this before. Those months following her brush with death was when their friendship had begun. But she couldn't rely on him now. He had enough problems. This time, she had to be the strong one.

Besides, for God's sake, she was a cop. She had stared down dealers, chased felons, subdued prisoners. Facing danger, living through it, learning to laugh it off—that was all part of the job.

So she tried to laugh, but a sound outside drew her startled gaze to the backdoor's curtained window. Had she locked the door when she came home? She started forward to check when the next-door neighbor's dog began to howl, and she stopped, seized by an unreasonable fear.

But she shook it off, thinking, *The guys at work would be laughing their butts off if they could see me now.* "Tough Girl Talbot. Woman of Steel," she muttered, recalling some of the labels her fellow officers had pinned on her after she had made a few difficult arrests. Some people might have resented the nicknames. Lisa had been smart enough to realize the harmless teasing meant she belonged.

Visualizing her friends in the department relaxed Lisa. Not everyone was going to believe the rumors. She knew there were some people she could count on. Smiling, she started to check the lock.

But at that moment someone rapped on the door.

And Tough Girl Talbot screamed.

Chapter Two

Lisa's scream blinded Will to anything but getting through the door. Later, he could only thank God it wasn't locked. Otherwise he might have torn it off the hinges and knocked his shoulder out of its socket.

But it wasn't locked. And in two seconds he was in the kitchen, his gun in his hand, ready for whatever threatened Lisa.

There was only her, however, white-faced, her hand over her mouth, staring at him as though he were an apparition.

"Jesus, Lisa, what—"

She didn't allow him to complete the words. She just stepped into his arms.

Vaguely he was aware of Terry running in from the front of the house, yelling. He felt the boy's arms lock around Lisa's waist from the other side. He heard Lisa repeating over and over, "It's okay, I'm okay." But his most vivid impression was of the way her slender shoulders shook. He had held her just this way after Mickey died. He hadn't touched her since. Disturbed by the memory, he tried to draw away, but she clung all the tighter.

"Lisa," he murmured, turning his face into her sweet-smelling hair. "What is it? Why did you scream?"

She shook her head and at last allowed him to step back. He kicked the backdoor shut and leaned against it while Lisa turned to gather her frightened son in her arms.

"What's wrong?" Terry was asking.

There was a tremble in his mother's voice. "I just got scared."

"Did Will—"

"Will just knocked on the door," she said, and drew a deep breath. Color was beginning to return to her cheeks as she looked at Will.

In the middle of slipping his gun back into the shoulder holster beneath his jacket, he paused. "I knocked on the door and you screamed? Jesus, Lisa—"

"It was a reflex," she cut in.

"You don't just scream on reflex."

Her gaze faltered under his. "I was about to lock the door when you knocked. I didn't expect anyone to be out there."

Terry spoke up, "Will always comes in this door, Mom. Don't you remember?"

She smiled down at the boy. "Now I do."

"Anyway," he continued, moving from his mother to Will. "I'm glad it was you."

Will started to ruffle Terry's hair, but remembered just in time that such gestures were no longer welcomed by this nine but-going-on-nineteen boy. He put out his hand instead. "Good to see you, *amigo.*"

They went through the elaborate handshake ritual so beloved to small boys who are trying to be cool. Then Terry's eyes, as deep blue as Lisa's, grew solemn. With his adult candor, which had often astounded Will, he said, "I'm really sorry Uncle Mickey is dead."

Stiffening, Will flashed a look at Lisa, then back to Terry. How was he supposed to reply?

Terry's earnestness gave way to uncertainty as he glanced at his mother, too. "Wasn't I supposed to say anything?"

The guilt in the boy's voice made Will speak up before Lisa could reply. "Of course you can say that. I told you before that you can say anything to me." Without hesitation this time, he touched the boy's cheek and was rewarded by a beaming smile.

"Come on," Terry said then, tugging Will toward the living room. "Mom got me a new game cartridge last week."

"I'll make you both a snack," Lisa said.

Will paused beside her. "We're going to talk about that scream," he promised. Before she could answer he followed Terry down the hall, shedding his jacket and holster on the way.

But there was no chance for adult conversation in the next few hours. Terry was bubbling over with everything that had happened to him in the week since he had last seen Will. Lisa stayed in the background. The pleasure the boy took in being with him made Will feel guiltier than ever about staying away for the past week. Terry's father, although prompt with his child payment checks, had severed all contact with his son after he moved to the West Coast nearly eight years ago. Will wondered how any man could walk away from his child. Rich Talbot was missing out, and in the last few years, Will had been glad to fill in the empty spaces in Terry's life.

Tonight, Will gave Terry his undivided attention. He got a lot out of the exchange. In truth, these were the first waking moments since Mickey's death that Will had been able to relax.

He had always felt at ease here in Lisa's home. The house was a simple Greek revival cottage, fairly new in construction but classically Southern in style. The living and dining rooms were on one side of the downstairs, Lisa's bedroom and bath on the other. Terry's room and another small bedroom occupied the second half story. The kitchen and adjoining deck stretched across the back, while a wide, columned porch embraced the front. Like Will's Aunt Elena, Lisa had the ability to make what was most simple into a welcoming retreat. The colors were the secret, he thought, deep greens and blues, with furniture that was easy on a man's tired muscles.

By the time Terry astounded his mother by asking to be tucked in, Will was feeling better than he had in days. But the "tucking in" entreaty was a delay tactic Will recognized from his own childhood. Terry took his time getting into his pajamas while insisting on several time-outs to show Will a couple dozen new treasures—an odd-shaped rock he and a friend had dug from a nearby stream, the picture of a fighter plane he had cut from a magazine.

However, when model cars, balls and assorted little boy debris had been cleared from his bed, Terry settled willingly under the sheets. But he still wasn't ready to sleep. He kept asking questions. Did Will think he could make the basketball team? What was Will's opinion on snakes as pets? Did Will think Lisa would up his allowance? The queries followed each other hard and fast until Will had to become firm.

"Your mother is going to kill us both if you don't go to sleep," he said, reaching for the switch on the bedside lamp. But Terry's last question made him pause.

"Are you sad about Uncle Mickey?"

He should have known he couldn't escape the reality of his life, not even for an evening spent with a little boy. Leaving the light on, Will sat down on the edge of the narrow bed.

"Mom said you were sad," Terry continued. "She said that's why you hadn't been over to see us. But you don't look so sad to me."

Will was grateful Terry couldn't see into the dark, hollow recesses of his heart. "Sometimes a person can just be sad inside."

The boy considered that for a moment. "I guess Uncle Mickey was that way."

"Why do you say that?"

"When I asked Mom why he died, she said he had a lot of problems and decided he didn't want to be alive anymore."

"That's right."

Terry frowned, his gaze intent on Will's face. "But every time I was with him, he was always laughing and telling me jokes. What kind of problems did he have?"

How did Will explain duplicity and betrayal to Terry, especially when he didn't understand it himself. "I guess it's like we said before, he didn't let anyone know how bad he was feeling."

"I liked him," Terry said with the simple logic of a child. "I still don't see why he would want to die."

There was more Will didn't understand, a lot more. And he had no answers for Terry's innocent questions. Feeling awkward, he drew the spaceship-patterned sheets up to Terry's chin. "Go to sleep. Stop worrying about Mickey."

"But I liked him," Terry insisted, yawning.

"He liked you, too," Will replied, although he wasn't sure if it was true. Who knew the real feelings Mickey had hidden behind his wide, easy smile?

"I heard Mom and Andy say he did some bad things."

"Don't think about that. Think about the good stuff he did." Will clicked off the lamp. "Now go to sleep."

Obediently, Terry snuggled down and turned on his side. Will squeezed the boy's shoulder as he stood. "Be brave, *amigo*." The words slipped out so effortlessly that it was a moment before Will realized it was the same phrase Mickey had often said to him when he was a child.

The utter waste of it all, the loss, stabbed him suddenly, and he turned from the bed, eager to flee the memories. Lisa was standing in the doorway, silhouetted by the light from the second-story landing. Will was certain she had heard his conversation with Terry. She said nothing, however, as they left the room and went downstairs.

At the foot of the staircase in the living room, she touched Will's arm. "Thank you for talking to him."

Not looking at her, he crossed the room to where his leather jacket and holster lay across the back of a wing chair. "It was nothing."

She followed him. "You were honest with him. That's what he needed."

"I didn't say anything you didn't tell him yourself."

"He wanted to hear it from you."

"I don't know why."

"Because you're important to him. And Mickey—"

"I don't want to talk about Mickey," Will said harshly as he shrugged into his shoulder holster.

"But we have to."

"No, we don't." Snatching up his jacket, he turned to face her. "It would suit me fine if I never heard his name again."

She fell back a step, and her delicate eyebrows drew together in a frown. "I gather you're not taking the advice you gave Terry."

"What do you mean?"

"You told him to remember the good stuff about Mickey. What are you going to remember?"

"Terry is a little boy who happened to think Mickey was a great guy. I'm not willing to disillusion him so completely yet. He'll find out the truth one day, anyway."

"You loved Mickey, too. That can't have disappeared."

Anger unfurled inside Will, replacing the loss he had felt upstairs with Terry. He was glad. The anger was an emotion with which he was far more comfortable. He glared at Lisa. "A lot of things disappeared the minute I saw Mickey holding that gun on you."

"That one moment can't replace all he meant to you."

Will held up his hand to silence her. "Could we just *not* analyze my feelings about this?"

"But you need to talk to someone, to let all this out."

"Forget it, Lisa."

"Well, if you don't want to discuss it with me, then talk to Andy or Dr. Hastings—"

"The staff shrink?"

She stiffened at his tone. "And what would be wrong with that? As you've said yourself about a hundred times, when people have a problem—"

"But that's just it," Will retorted. "I don't have a problem. I don't need to get in touch with my feelings. I don't need to sort anything out. I understand exactly how I feel."

Lisa stared at him in silence. She had never heard Will speak with such rage. It was eating him up, would destroy him if he didn't deal with it. But she couldn't force him to talk. She could only be here for him if and when he ever decided to open up.

She took a deep, steadying breath and conceded, "All right, Will. I'm not going to push you about this."

"Good." He looked down at his jacket and then tossed it back onto the chair. "We still have some talking to do. About what happened when I knocked on the door."

With elaborate care, Lisa pushed up the sleeves of her gray sweatshirt. "There's nothing to say. I've been wound up all day long, and you startled me."

"You don't normally startle so easily."

Lisa didn't want to tell him that she didn't feel normal these days. Whatever she might say would lead them straight back to the subject of Mickey, and Will would become angry again. She dismissed the subject with a wave of her hand. Not bothering to see what Will thought, she crossed the living room, sat down in front of the television set and began stowing Terry's video games in the cabinet where they belonged.

Will followed her and took a seat on the edge of the coffee table. His scrutiny of her movements made her so nervous she sat back on her heels, her hands clenched in her lap.

"You're as tight as a wound top," Will said.

"I'm just tired."

"The hell you are. Now tell me what's really going on with you."

She folded her arms across her chest. "Why is it that you can be tense and edgy and I'm not allowed to ask about it, but you can give me the third degree?"

"I'm not the one who screamed bloody murder when someone knocked on the door." The muscles worked in his throat as he swallowed. "I'm not the one who was almost killed."

"I thought we weren't going to talk about Mickey."

He muttered a curse and shot to his feet. "I guess there's nothing we can discuss that doesn't involve him. I wish to God he had checked out a little earlier. It would have saved us all a lot of grief."

Stumbling to her feet, Lisa grabbed his arm. "You don't mean that."

He shook her off. "I do, too."

She caught him again, forced him to turn to her. He flinched, and she hesitated. Countless times she had touched Will without thinking, without having to wonder how he would react. She would be damned if that spontaneity was going to be lost to them now. She framed his face with her hands, and surprisingly, he didn't pull away. "Will, please," she murmured. "Let me help you with this."

For a moment they were together, locked in the sweet harmony they had known before this nightmare began. The communion lasted only a second, however, before Will turned from her again.

His shoulders sloped wearily as he dragged a hand through his dark hair. His voice was choked. "I just can't, Lisa."

In answer, she slipped her hand in his. He was still half turned from her, but his fingers threaded through hers and clung.

"Today was almost more than I could take," he muttered. "Having to go through it all again, tell them what he said, what he did, what almost happened to you."

"I know," she whispered. "It was hell for me, too."

He looked at her. "They put you through the same thing?"

"They glossed over the night Mickey died. It was the other questions that got me."

"What other questions?"

"The ones about all those stupid rumors."

He still looked puzzled. "Rumors?"

Too late, Lisa realized Will might not have been asked the same questions, he might not realize the extent of the talk circulating through the department. She started trying to hedge, "I guess what I meant was—"

"What rumors?" he pressed, taking her by the shoulders. "Are you talking about those stories that slob Robbins is spreading? I.A. asked you about that?"

She knew he would see through whatever lie she told him. Quickly, remaining as unemotional as possible, she relayed what Andy had told her and what the I.A. panel had asked. Will paced away from her and stood, his head slightly bowed, as she talked. To give him credit, he didn't interrupt, didn't explode, didn't do anything but listen.

She ended by telling him the warning Andy had issued. "He's way off base, I think. No one is going to come after any of us to try and keep us quiet. Anybody out there with a guilty conscience has got to figure we've spilled our guts to I.A. by now."

"But that's why you're so damn jumpy," Will said, his dark eyes glittering dangerously.

She shrugged. "So I got a little skittish."

"A little?"

"So I screamed," Lisa admitted, irritation beginning to edge through her concern for him. "It's not the first time I've been startled. It won't be the last. Stop making such a big deal about it."

"But you're frightened. In the safety of our own house, you're scared to death. That's a big deal to me."

"I'm not scared to death," she denied. "I've been taking care of myself and Terry for a long time, and it will take more than some vague suspicion of Andy's to really rattle me now. I've been through worse, Will. You know I have."

Will's face set in hard, bitter lines. "Oh, yeah, Lisa, you've been through worse. After all, you've looked down the barrel of Mickey Vallejo's gun."

She held her head high. "Looked down it and survived."

"Don't tell me you don't still feel it."

"Will—"

"Don't tell me you weren't afraid, aren't still afraid." Will stepped forward and grasped her shoulders, giving her a little shake. "You can't lie to me, Lisa. I know you too well."

"Of course I was afraid. And maybe I'm still jumpy, but that isn't the end of the world. I'm not going to let any of this get to me."

Will's eyes softened. His hand slipped from her shoulder to her face, and his thumb stroked gently down her jawline. "I don't want you to go through what you did before."

She knew he referred to three years ago, after she had been shot. "I won't," she whispered. "I'm too tough to fall apart. You should know that better than anyone else."

Will leaned forward, and Lisa waited for his lips to touch hers. But he didn't kiss her. With a soft exclamation, he pulled away. Again the moment was lost; their closeness shattered. And once more, Lisa saw fury claim his features.

"Damn, Mickey," he muttered. "He died by his own hand, and that means eternal hell, but even that seems too good for him now. He could still ruin our lives."

"Only if we let him."

"And how do you propose that we stop it? Because of him, because of *me,* you and Andy are under suspicion. God, Lisa, I can't tell you how sorry I am."

The utter despair in his voice shook her. "None of this is your fault. Stop thinking that way right now. Hate Mickey if you have to, but don't blame yourself."

"But neither you nor Andy have ever even considered doing anything wrong, and now you're being investigated by Internal Affairs."

"I don't know that there's a full-blown investigation—"

"And what were those questions they asked you today? It sounds like an investigation to me." He passed a hand over his face. "None of this would be happening if not for your relationship with Mickey or me."

"Eventually everyone will know we didn't do anything. The rumors will stop."

"We hope," Will said skeptically.

"We have to believe the truth will win out in the end."

Shaking his head, Will stalked to the chair, grabbed up his jacket again. "I'm not sure what the truth is anymore."

"Yes, you do."

But Will wasn't listening to her. He shrugged into his jacket and with a hand on the front doorknob, said, "Lock this after me, Lisa. Put on your burglar alarm, and be careful. I'm not so sure Andy's suspicions are wrong."

"I wish you wouldn't go like this."

"I have things to do. I have to check on Elena. I have to...to think, to..." His words trailed away as he jerked the door open.

Lisa caught up with him at the edge of her front porch. "Stay with me tonight."

He hesitated. "I thought you weren't afraid."

"That's not why I want you here."

He looked at her then, his face clearly visible in the pool of light from the lamp beside her front door, but his expression was unreadable.

Lisa had never pleaded with Will for anything, but she didn't want him to walk away from her tonight. Somehow, some way, they had to form a connection. The longer this distance between them was allowed to exist, the deeper it would become. Taking a deep breath, she caught his hand in hers again. "I've missed you, Will. I want you to stay with me tonight."

He lifted a hand to her hair, and in his eyes she could see the yearning. But it was quickly banked. He shook his head, muttered, "I've gotta go." Not looking back, he disappeared around the corner of the house to the driveway where his car was parked.

Shivering in the cool air, she waited until the powerful engine of his black Camaro roared to life. But she didn't watch him leave. She went inside, locked the door, and secured her snug little house against whatever unnamed terrors the world outside might hold.

Atlanta, like most large cities, moved fast, propelled by the crowded highways that looped in ever-widening circles around its metropolitan sprawl. On this cool November evening, Will was glad to be on one of those roads. He pushed his car forward with a heavy foot on the accelerator. Out here, he was just one more swift-moving car, blending with a thousand others. He wasn't Mickey's nephew, Terry's father figure, or Lisa's lover. Here, he could crank up his stereo and lose himself in Jerry Lee Lewis's piano.

But Will had never driven a road without having a destination in mind. He wanted to run away, but when the exit to Elena's northeastern Atlanta home came into sight, he obediently sent the Camaro down the ramp.

No lights showed in the sprawling ranch-style house as he pulled into the drive. He killed the motor and sat for a moment, trying to decide if he should go or stay. The decision was made for him when the light over the front door came on. If he had awakened Elena by driving up, it would do no good to leave now.

His diminutive aunt met him at the door, leaning heavily on her cane, her dark eyes concerned. "You said you were going to Lisa's, so I didn't expect you back tonight."

He pressed a kiss to her cheek. "What are you doing out of your wheelchair? I thought the doctor—"

Her black eyes snapped. "He can go rot. I felt like walking."

The sassy tone was typical for the woman who had fought rheumatoid arthritis for much of her adult life. The disease that had twisted her joints had never touched her spirit. But it took all of Will's control not to assist her as she shuffled and struggled from the door to the wheelchair that waited nearby. She did allow him to help her sit down. With a push of a button, she sent the chair forward into the den at the rear of the house.

He followed in her wake, snapping on lights. "You should be in bed, Aunt Elena."

"Why? I wouldn't be sleeping."

"Elena—"

"A better question is why you're here instead of at Lisa's."

He avoided answering by settling into his favorite leather recliner. "Where's Marta?" He referred to Elena's long-time housekeeper.

"I told her to go home. There's no need for her to stay here every night."

"But how would you have managed?"

She lifted her head as high as her affliction allowed. "I'm not completely helpless yet, Will."

"I just don't like to think of you sitting here by yourself. When I told you I was going to Lisa's, you said Marta would be here."

Elena sighed. "I knew you wouldn't go if you knew I would be alone, but quite frankly, much as I love you, I wanted some time to myself."

"Time to sit alone in the dark?"

"Time to try and make some sense of a few things."

For the first time Will noticed the papers piled on the coffee table. There were stacks of bank statements and a few other official-looking documents, all arranged in the neat fashion he would expect from Elena. He shook his head at her. "I told you not to worry about this."

"I lost my husband, not my mind."

"I never said you weren't capable of handling this. I just didn't want you to have to go through it."

Her gnarled fingers plucked at the folds of her black skirt. "I had to face it," she murmured. "I had to see how much he took." Her chin trembled, but her voice remained steady. "It had to be a lot, Will. We didn't have money for the things he bought. He must have paid in cash for most of them. I don't know why I was foolish enough not to suspect what was happening. How could I have been so blind?"

Will didn't vent his anger against Mickey. Despite what his uncle had done, he couldn't bring himself to verbalize his feelings to Elena.

Elena's head bowed. Her hair, coiled in a smooth bun at the nape of her neck, was still thick and black, touched with gray only at her temples. "It's funny," she said, "But a little while ago, when I heard your car, I was thinking so hard about Mickey that I thought it was his car. For a minute I forgot." She looked up at Will. "I forgot everything. And then..." She bit her lip, unable to go on.

He knelt beside her chair, one hand covering hers. "This is why you shouldn't sit alone in the dark."

She managed a slight smile. "People go crazy with the lights on, too, you know."

"You're not going crazy."

"Sometimes I wish I could." She drew in a ragged breath and appeared to regain her equilibrium. "I'm glad you're here, Will. I don't know what I would do without you."

"I'm going to take care of you."

Her hand moved under his. "When your father left you and your mother here in Atlanta, he came to me and Mickey, and he asked us to look after you, should anything happen to him." Her gaze seemed to rove over Will's features. "You look like your father, Will. But then, the men in our family have always been handsome."

Despite their shared pain, they managed to laugh together before Will said, "You looked after me pretty well, you know."

"Then I guess the caring, the responsibility comes full circle," she said. "But I don't want to burden you, Will."

"The family circle could never be a burden."

"Now you sound like Mickey."

Avoiding her gaze, Will stood and slipped off his jacket and holster. Family, honor, reputation—all were principles his uncle had preached long and hard. The pity was, he had never learned the lessons he had taught.

"How was Lisa?" Elena asked, giving Will a reason not to reply to her comment about Mickey.

"Okay, I guess."

"And why didn't you stay?"

"I wanted to check on you."

Elena tsk-tsked. "Lisa is good for you, Will. She and Terry both."

He ignored her and crossed the room to the piano in the corner. "Why don't I play you something? Maybe then you'll sleep."

"Your mother would be happy that those piano lessons weren't wasted."

Will sat down and ran his hands over the smooth ivory keys. He had taken the lessons because his mother insisted, had practiced to please her, had missed baseball games and taken his share of ribbing from other boys. Only as an adult had he learned to love coaxing music from the keyboard.

"Play my favorite," Elena commanded, wheeling closer.

The opening chords of "Over the Rainbow" filled the room, filled Will's head. Somehow he managed to lose himself in the music. One note melted into the next. "Rainbow" blended into "Yesterday" into "Our Love is Here to Stay."

The melodies washed through him while, unbidden, Lisa's words came back. *Stay with me,* she had said.

And he had walked away. With his head full of throbbing, haunting melodies, he couldn't remember why. As Elena had done earlier tonight, he forgot his troubles.

While the final notes played out beneath his hands, Will glanced at his aunt. Her face was wet with tears.

And he remembered why he had left Lisa, why even looking at her brought him pain too harsh to bear.

To his great sorrow, he remembered everything.

* * *

Lisa had given up trying to sleep, had even given up on the novel she had found so spellbinding only a few weeks ago. As the clock on her fireplace mantel struck midnight, she sat down on her living room couch and reached for the television remote. But the telephone rang instead. She snatched the receiver from the end table. The caller hung up when she spoke.

A rude wrong number. A teenager playing a prank. There were many explanations. There was no reason to get nervous.

Firmly, Lisa set the phone back in its cradle. "I refuse to read anything into this," she told the empty room. Instead she sat back on the couch and drew her favorite, soft wool comforter around her. Though the material warmed her, it was a poor substitute for what she really craved.

Her face grew warm as she remembered asking Will to stay with her tonight. The embarrassment was silly, of course. The honesty of her relationship with Will had always pleased her. From the beginning, even when they were just friends, they hadn't played games with each other. So that when they became lovers, there was no pretense, no reason for either of them to be less than up-front about their expectations or needs. They had come together so naturally, so easily. A few weeks ago Lisa wouldn't have been embarrassed to ask Will to stay.

Snuggling deeper into the comforter, she thought about the first night they had made love. A hot August night. Had it been only four months since then? Somehow, perhaps because Will had been part of her life for several years, it seemed they had been intimate for much longer.

It had started in this room. Terry had been away, spending the night with the family of his favorite sitter. Lisa and Will had been racking up the overtime, trying to get a lead in the police corruption probe. Officially, they were both assigned to a prostitution crackdown unit. In reality, they were studying their fellow officers in the district, watching for signs of graft. Their official assignment was a success; their real intent was leaving them empty-handed. They were both frustrated, but when rehashing the same ground for the tenth time that evening proved futile, Will had started to leave.

"I wish you wouldn't," Lisa said, refilling his coffee mug and holding it out. "You know you're just going to go home and think about this some more. And my coffee's always better than yours."

Will laughed, accepted the mug and settled back on the couch. "I think you just don't want to be alone in this empty house."

"You're right," she admitted ruefully. "It always feels funny when Terry's not safe and sound up in his room."

"When I was a boy, my mom said my empty room was like a hole in her heart." He grinned. "She was a little melodramatic."

"You don't talk much about her."

"I have some mixed emotions about Mother."

Lisa waited, not wanting to press, but interested in a subject he had rarely discussed. Most of the time, he was intensely private. Perhaps it was the quiet intimacy of the late hour, perhaps the trust between them had grown to a point where Will thought he could trust Lisa. Whatever the reason, he told her how his parents had met after his father had joined the air force.

"Someone like my mother probably shouldn't have married a man like Dad."

"How do you mean?"

"She was a real homebody, kind of frail, very shy. And Dad was this young pilot, the son of two Cuban immigrants, with a fire in his belly."

"A fire?"

"He was born here in the States, of course, and from what Mickey says, he was a real patriot. That's what sent him into the military."

"It couldn't have been easy to be of Cuban ancestry and serve in the armed forces at that point in time."

Will nodded. "Elena told me how hard some people made it on Dad. It was the same for Mickey. After Mickey's stint in the army, he had joined the police force in their hometown in north Florida. He had grown up there, but some people didn't trust him. Maybe that time was what made Mickey so determined to prove the stereotypes wrong. Not everyone who came from that island was a subversive or a cigar-smoking criminal. My grandparents were teachers. They raised Dad and Elena to be good people. Mickey grew up next door to them, his father was Cuban, his mother an Anglo. Elena says his mother's parents never forgave her for marrying a Hispanic."

"How terrible," Lisa murmured.

"Mickey says it was okay," Will replied. "Though it must have hurt to have your grandparents refuse to acknowledge you." He sighed. "I was luckier. My mother's mother, the only grandparent I ever knew, was good to me. Mother and I lived with her here in Atlanta when Dad did his first tour in Vietnam. We stayed on in the house after she died and after Dad didn't come back a second time."

Lisa had known his father had been shot down early in the Vietnam conflict. "You were only six, right? You must have been devastated."

"To tell you the truth, Dad had been gone so much, I barely knew him. It was Mother who couldn't recover from his death."

"What do you mean?"

He frowned, as if the memories were painful. "She had always been frail, and Dad's death just crushed her. She got pretty overprotective of me. She had to know where I was all the time. She was always telling me that I had to be the man of the house, that I had to protect her, that I had to be a hero like Dad. That's a pretty tall order for a little boy to fill."

Lisa sighed. She couldn't imagine placing a burden of such magnitude on Terry.

"I could have turned into a real little sissy," Will continued. "But Elena and Mickey moved to Atlanta to be near me. They were my escape. And when Mother died when I was eleven, I moved in with them."

"No wonder you care so much for them both."

"I owe them a lot." With restless motions, Will stood and crossed to the window, where he pushed the curtain aside and stared out at the night.

Several moments passed before Lisa softly called his name. She would never embarrass Will by pushing him to reveal more than he wanted, but he looked so bereft, so sad. She felt guilty for having pushed him to tell this much. "I didn't mean to pry."

"You didn't." Hands thrust into his jeans pockets, he turned and shrugged. "It's funny. A person can grow up, be in control of their life, be happy. And then sometimes it all comes back. Sometimes you close your eyes and you're this little kid again, lying in your bed, listening to a vine scratch against the side of the house, wondering how in the hell you're gonna be man enough to protect your mother."

Lisa didn't stop to consider her actions before she crossed the room to him. Aching for the frightened little boy he had been, she put her arms around the man. She hugged him in the way she might hug any friend who had shared some deep, private pain.

Then it all changed.

One minute they were two friends. The next his mouth was on hers. Before she could think, she was drawn into a kiss that deepened and grew. Forgotten was the comfort she had intended to give him; what remained was passion. Fiery, vibrating passion.

At long last, they drew apart in stunned surprise.

Then Will smiled. "I think I've been wondering how that would feel for a long, long time."

She was shaken by the strength of the kiss, but she followed his lighthearted lead, tipped her head back and grinned. "How did it feel, Lieutenant?"

He threaded his hand through her hair, pulling her back to him as he murmured, "I think I need more evidence before I can close the case."

So they kissed again. With a hunger devouring in its intensity. Until that moment Lisa hadn't realized she was starving for this man's touch.

She didn't remember anything else they'd said. She could only recall the teasing glide of Will's tongue against her own. Her shocked thrill of pleasure when he'd gathered her into his arms and kicked her bedroom door open. The vibration of his laughter as he'd pressed his face to the valley between her breasts. The corded steel of his muscles when he'd lifted her arching body high against his own.

That night had been wild—free of inhibitions, free of doubt. In the morning light, they had faced each other without fear. No promises had been made, no words of love exchanged. But that was fine with Lisa. She had given and received such words before. Will had, too. Neither one of them trusted words. Lisa preferred the ease of one day slipping into the next with Will. They had been so open with each other.

But now he had closed her out.

She sat alone in her living room, her body throbbing from the memory of his caresses. Strange how he had told her to lock the doors when he had left her tonight. The real danger lay in the barriers he was putting between them.

Chapter Three

While Lisa watched, leaves fell in a flurry of color outside Elena's greenhouse. Crimson, gold and orange. Yellow, green and brown. They swirled and danced across the yard, propelled by an insistent wind. Yesterday's warm sunshine had given way to overcast skies. Fittingly grim, Lisa thought as she turned from the scene outside and called, "Elena, where are you? Marta said you were out here."

"In the back," came a voice from the opposite end of the long, narrow room.

Lisa found the older woman working at a low wooden table. Surrounded by the riotous beauty of her beloved roses and plants, Elena looked pale and drawn, but her smile was bright. "It's good to see you, dear. I hope you brought Terry with you."

"He's out in the kitchen snitching cookies from Marta."

"I'm sure that makes her happy. My appetite doesn't suit her."

"You are too thin."

"Oh, please," Elena protested. "What do I do to work up an appetite?" Even as she spoke she was pulling yellow leaves from a large potted fern. As always, Lisa was amazed at the dexterity she coaxed from her crippled joints. Elena had always found ways to adapt. That ability should serve her well now.

Leaves blew against the glass-paneled sides of the room again. Elena looked up, murmuring, "Winter's on its way."

Lisa nodded, still following the motions of her hands. "I always hate to see the fall colors go. When I was a girl, I asked my mother why God made the trees stand out in the winter cold without their clothes."

Elena chuckled. "I've always thought you had the heart of a poet. Your outlook is wasted on police work."

"I guess you think Will should be playing piano on a concert stage."

"Not a stage, necessarily. Maybe some smoky little bar somewhere." The two women smiled at each other, but then Elena's tone grew wry. "I'm afraid nothing but police work would be exciting enough to hold Will's attention for long."

"You know yourself that police work isn't really exciting. Eighty percent of the time, you're either chasing down blind alleys or sitting around waiting for something to happen."

"But when it happens..." Elena bit her lip, her dark eyes reflecting her concern. "How are you, dear?"

Lisa knew the phrase was more than polite interest. Since Mickey's funeral, she and Elena had never been alone long enough to talk about what he had tried to do. She enfolded the woman's fingers with her own. "I'm fine, really I am."

In her characteristic spunky style, Elena clucked her disapproval. "You wouldn't tell me if you weren't fine, would you?"

She had Lisa there. "You do understand people."

"Oh, I've been fooled a few times."

The softly voiced statement touched Lisa's heart. She took a seat on a nearby potting bench in order to be on Elena's level. "I want to know how you are," she said. "And no evasions, please. I understand people pretty well, too."

Elena managed a slight smile. "I'm surviving. Minute into hour into day, I take them one at a time."

"That's the only sensible approach."

"I'll get through this the same way I've made it through everything else. It's Will I worry about."

Lisa sighed. "Me, too."

"He can be so hard on himself."

"Oh, yes, Will Espinoza enjoys carrying the weight of everyone else's troubles on his shoulders."

Elena gave a distinctly unladylike snort. "It's his silly mother's fault. God rest her soul. She leaned on him far too much. It's not like me to speak so ill of the dead, Lisa, but I wish I had followed my impulses a time or two and slapped Kathy Espinoza's pretty face."

The vision of tiny Elena physically assaulting anyone amused Lisa. "I take it Will's mother wasn't your favorite person."

"My brother must have been distracted by a swively pair of hips and some long eyelashes or he wouldn't have saddled himself with such a useless creature."

"She did give us Will."

"Yes, childbirth was her one accomplishment," Elena agreed. "And she stopped at one child. My God, if I could have had children, I'd have tried for at least ten."

"And no doubt organized them into a baseball team." Besides her house and her plants, the Atlanta Braves baseball team was one of Elena's passions.

"Nine players and a spare." Her eyes flashed with unabashed pleasure. "Mickey used to say—" She broke off before completing the statement.

Lisa patted her arm. "It's okay. You can talk about him to me. I don't mind."

Elena seemed more fragile than ever as she sagged back in her chair. "Will minds. He'll barely say Mickey's name."

"He has a lot of healing to do."

"He's so angry." Elena sat forward again, her gaze intent on Lisa's. "Help him. Please."

"You know I will if he'll let me."

"If I know you, you'll find a way to reach him. I just hope he knows what a prize he has in you."

"I'm not such a prize."

"Now, now," Elena remonstrated. "No false modesty, please. The minute you walked into this house, I told Marta you were the one for Will. You're strong enough to stand eye to eye with him. I helped raise him, so I know he can be stubborn and egotistical and hard to fathom."

"And here I always thought you were such a doting aunt."

"In a family full of strong men, I've had to be realistic rather than sentimental." Elena's mouth tightened. "Just don't make the mistake of coddling Will. You need to push him a little from time to time, shake him out of his unyielding ways. Why, if you had prodded him some, it might not have taken years for you two to get together."

"We were friends," Lisa protested.

Elena's raised eyebrow was an eloquent commentary on Will and Lisa's friendship, a subject she had discussed on several other occasions. She didn't elaborate now, but grew serious again, instead. "I meant what I said, Lisa. Will needs you to get through this. Don't give up on him."

"I wouldn't do that."

"He'll push you away again and again."

Thinking of the way he had walked out on her last night, Lisa nodded. Elena was right. And it was one thing for her to say she wouldn't allow Will to push her away permanently. It was another to actually do it.

"I guess I've lectured you enough for one afternoon," Elena said. With her forearm, she raked the dead leaves from the table to a trashcan below. She nodded toward the far corner. "Come over here and look at my yellow roses."

The flowers she indicated filled a large square table, their blossoms ranging in color from the palest ivory to a deep ocher.

"They're heavenly," Lisa said, standing back to admire the effect.

Elena's gaze softened. "I'm going to miss them."

"When the blooms fade?"

"When I leave."

Lisa didn't understand. "You're leaving?"

"Of course, I'll have to sell the house."

Sell her home? The very idea affronted Lisa. She knew how much the rambling brick house meant to Elena. Her zest for life and unflagging spirit were reflected in every corner. "You can't want to sell," she said in protest.

"What I want and what I have to do are two very different matters. Besides..." Elena glanced around the room, the happiness brought by the flowers fading from her expression. "How can I continue to take joy in this place now that I know how he paid for it?"

Lisa could see her point, but she still didn't like to think of Elena leaving here. The house was equipped to make her life more comfortable and wouldn't be easy or inexpensive to duplicate elsewhere.

"This morning I told the nurse who comes every day not to come back," Elena continued. "I'm trying to economize."

"But how will you manage?"

"Marta will stay. She's so loyal. She's going to let her apartment go and move in here for a while. She says she'll go with me no matter where I move."

"She's a good friend."

Once more, shadows clouded the older woman's face. "She's one of my few friends."

"But you have more friends than anyone I know."

"You're talking about the wives of the officers Mickey served with all these years?" She shook her head. "Already they've stopped coming around. Not all of them, of course. There are some who aren't afraid. But none of them know what to say. And no one wants to be touched by the scandal."

Suddenly furious, Lisa thought of all the parties Elena had thrown for Mickey's co-workers. The backyard barbecues. The Halloween costume extravaganzas. How many young police wives had gone to Elena for support when they felt the pressures of their mates' jobs? What about the men and women officers who, upset about one matter or another, had come home with Mickey, pulled a chair up to Elena's table, slept in her guest room? How many benefits had she organized? How many Thanksgivings and Christmases had this house been filled to overflowing? Elena's disintegrating physical health had limited the places she could go, but her door had always been open to the members of the police family.

Lisa was incensed to think that family was turning its back on Elena now. Incensed and disillusioned. She had thought better of most of her co-workers.

"Don't be angry," Elena said, accurately reading Lisa's expression. "Right now, everyone is wondering who knew what Mickey was doing, who was in on it with him. In the end, they all have to look out for their own lives and jobs and paychecks."

"You shouldn't be punished for what he did."

Before more could be said, Terry bounded down the glass-enclosed walkway that joined the greenhouse to Elena's den. Throwing open the door, he demanded, "Are you guys gonna stay out here forever?"

"Where are your manners?" Lisa rebuked evenly. "You know you don't run in someone else's house."

Elena chuckled. "I'm glad he feels at home. If I could run, I assure you I'd gallop from room to room."

Terry grinned at her in gratitude. "Will's here. We've both been eatin' cookies with Marta."

"So I see." Lisa brushed some crumbs from his cheek.

"Aw, Mom."

"Please tell Will to come out here," Elena told Terry. While he scrambled to do so, she turned back to Lisa. "Don't tell Will what I'm planning to do about the house."

"He'll have to know."

"Of course. Just not now."

Lisa understood. In all the ways that mattered, this was Will's childhood home. He wasn't by any stretch of the imagination an overly sentimental man, but to see this house go right now would be just one more loss.

As she watched him follow Terry into the greenhouse, Lisa thought Will looked tired. But earlier in the day, her own mirror had given testimony to the sleepless nights she had been experiencing. There was no reason to expect Will would be doing any better.

He bent and kissed his aunt, then nodded at Lisa without really meeting her gaze. "How are you?"

"Just fine." Lisa's voice sounded just a little too bright, even to her own ears. "Since I don't have to go back to work until Monday, I picked Terry up at school and we decided to pay Elena a visit."

"I'm sure she appreciates that."

The conversation was inane, impersonal, and Lisa was aware of the disapproving glance Elena directed at Will.

The older woman cleared her throat. "Terry, do you remember those baseball cards of Will's I promised you?"

"The ones he had when he was my age?"

"Marta found them when she was cleaning out the attic a few weeks ago. Why don't we go look them over?"

The boy's eyes brightened as he looked up at Will. "Are you sure I can have them?"

Will nodded, and Elena and Terry disappeared into the house. The woman was grinning, clearly pleased with her rather obvious ploy to leave Will and Lisa alone.

Lisa forced a light note into her voice and turned to survey the roses again. "Are you sure you want to give away those cards? They might be valuable."

"Then maybe he can sell them someday and pay for medical school."

"Medical school? Something tells me he might turn out to be a cop."

"Let's hope to God not."

The bitterness in his voice made her look up, but one glance at his shuttered expression convinced her any arguments about the merits of law enforcement were pointless. At least now.

He broke the sudden, strained silence. "Have you been reassigned?"

"I'm supposed to see Captain Hardiman on Monday morning. I'm sure I'll get the news then."

"I saw him today."

"And?" Lisa prompted when he didn't elaborate. "Where's your new assignment?"

His reply was clipped. "Back on patrol. First shift. West side."

Lisa was surprised. Although the assignment wasn't a demotion, it seemed an unusual choice for someone of Will's abilities. Patrol work was the lifeblood of any police department. Detectives and special units might get all the glory in the press and were glamorized on TV, but it was the policemen who patrolled the city's neighborhoods who were the front line of defense against crime. Everyone started as a patrolman, many preferred to stay there. But Will had worked on a special Narcotics Task Force, in Homicide and then in I.A. To put him back on patrol seemed a waste.

Or a punishment.

Or simply the best place to watch him.

"The captain wanted me to take some time off," he added when she didn't make a comment. "I told him, no thanks."

"Maybe it wouldn't have been such a bad idea."

"Will you take time off if he offers it?"

Lisa thought of sitting home, wondering what everyone in the department might be saying or thinking about her role in Mickey's death. No, she understood Will's need to be at work.

His next harsh words echoed her thoughts. "No way am I going to stay away while everyone I ever thought was a friend is whispering behind my back."

"Not everyone—"

"Oh yeah? This morning, I was edgy, knowing I had to see Hardiman. So I went down to the gym to shoot a few. I walk in the locker room, there were two guys in there. We were all rookies together. But they shut up when they see me. I walk into headquarters and everyone's looking, you know, but trying not to look. I should give my chiropractor some of their names. He could rake it in treating them for whiplash."

Lisa smiled. Such sardonic humor was more Will's normal mode. "You ought to get some of his cards, take them in—"

"And maybe I can find a good proctologist for the I.A. panel."

That surprised her. "Did they call you in again?"

He grunted in reply. "Bunch of tight—"

"What did they want?" she cut in.

"They gave me the same drill you and Andy got yesterday. What did I know about Mickey's activities and when did I know it? I guess they waited to ask me because they figured I couldn't handle everything in one day."

"To give them the benefit of a doubt, maybe they really were trying to be kind."

His eyes widened in astonishment. "Since when are you Little Miss Lisa Sunshine?"

She bit back a sharp retort. "I'm not going to fight with you, Will."

"Oh really? Then maybe you could answer a question or two."

"What?"

Feet apart, he braced his hands on his hips and glared at her. "A couple of their questions cleared up some of my own thinking. I guess I've been in a fog this past week, because I never thought to question why you went to that girl's apartment alone the night Mickey died."

"But I've told everyone why," Lisa said, not sure why he was questioning her actions. "I didn't want to tell you anything about Mickey until I felt the woman was telling the truth. She was a hooker with a history of drug use. I had to be certain she wasn't just someone Mickey had busted who had an ax to grind. I wasn't going to make accusations without being sure."

"I was your partner," Will insisted. "You should have told me the minute you suspected Mickey."

"I couldn't hurt you like that until I had proof."

"Is that the real reason you didn't call me?"

"Will, I said—"

"Or was it because you didn't trust me?"

Shocked, she fell back a step. His accusation hurt more than his anger or his walking away last night. What was happening to him, to *them*, that he would think she could ever distrust him?

"Were you afraid I would warn him?"

Hard on her hurt came anger. She was so mad, she couldn't formulate a reply. Instead she pushed past him. At the edge of the room, his voice made her stop.

"I need to know, Lisa."

She measured her words carefully. "If you don't believe what I told you, if I have to justify my actions..." To her consternation, her voice shook, but she managed to steady it. "I'm not going to dignify your question with an answer."

"But I have a right—"

"No, you don't have a right," she cried, wheeling to face him again. "You have no right to reduce our relationship, our friendship, to this."

"I'm not reducing—"

"Oh, but you are. It's funny, Will. You're wondering if I trusted you. But if you trusted me, you wouldn't have to ask this question."

The door to the house slammed shut behind her while Will stood unmoving. Far off, he could hear Lisa calling for Terry and Elena. He wasn't going to wait around for the boy's goodbyes or his aunt's sharp-eyed glances. So he banged out the side door and went to his car.

He was in his condominium on the other side of the city before he realized it was the second time in as many days that he and Lisa had parted in anger. Well, no, that wasn't exactly right. Last night she hadn't been angry. She had been hurt by his refusal to stay. Today he had hurt her again by questioning her trust. And she was right. He should know better. He knew that in his head. But in his heart... Dear God, right now he questioned everything.

He stalked into his kitchen, grabbed a beer from the refrigerator and downed it in three gulps. His hand was on a second can when he realized what he was doing.

He didn't drink like this. He knew too many police officers who poured alcohol on their troubles in an effort to work them out. All they accomplished was adding fuel to the blaze, as Mickey used to say.

"Damn," Will muttered. Was there any way he was going to live the rest of his life without constant reminders of Mickey? A rough-edged defiance scraping his gut, he snatched up the remainder of the six-pack and carried it with him into the living room.

Several hours later, three of the five cans remained in a pool of condensation on his coffee table. The two empties had been flattened between his hands and thrown on the tiled fireplace hearth. And Will wasn't feeling any better than when he had sprawled on his couch. He was almost glad when the doorbell rang. But a glance through the peephole nearly sent him back to the beer.

"I know you're there," Andy called from outside. "Your car's outside, and your big, clumsy feet made too much noise coming to the door."

Muttering an oath, Will threw open the door and walked away without saying a word.

"Yes, thank you for asking me in," Andy said with heavy sarcasm. He closed the door and moved into the living room, where he set a pizza carton on the table next to the beer. "And yes, Will, it's nice to see you, too."

Will sat down on the couch again. "If you expected hospitality, you came to the wrong place."

Andy shrugged out of his navy sport coat and loosened his tie. "You could at least say thanks for the pizza."

"I didn't ask you for it."

"I can see you had a much more nutritious dinner in mind." Andy lifted the dripping beer by one of the empty plastic rings. "Hasn't anyone ever told you these plastic things are a danger to wildlife? Birds get their beaks caught in them and can't eat."

Will had had enough of the chitchat. "Say what you have to say, all right, Baskin. Then you can go home to your wife and kids and talk to them about environmental issues."

"Meg and the kids are at her parents' for the evening. I felt like pizza, and I swung by here to see if you wanted to share it."

"Right, like Lisa didn't tell you—"

"I haven't talked to her since yesterday. What should she have told me?"

Will couldn't doubt Andy's sincerity; the man never had been able to lie. His honesty was exceeded only by his tenacity, so getting him to leave would be wasted effort. Telling himself to chill out, Will took a deep breath and sat forward, reaching for the pizza. "So what's on this, anyway? I hope you got extra cheese."

"We weren't partners for a year without me learning something about you." Andy disappeared into the kitchen. He returned with a roll of paper towels, tore off a couple, then dropped them to the table. "I see these are recycled, Espinoza. Meg might forgive you for the plastic rings."

"I think your wife is overly concerned with the greening of the planet."

"There's something about having children that makes you think about the future." Andy grinned around a bite of pizza. "By the way, we're having another one."

It didn't register for a minute. Will just sat there, chewing his own pizza and frowning at his friend.

"Another baby," Andy elaborated as he took a seat in a nearby chair.

Will nearly choked. "A third one?"

"Hey, it surprised us, too. But you know how these things seem to creep up on Meg and me."

Will considered that an understatement. Nearly four years ago, Andy and Meg had been divorced from each other. Divorced, but not uninvolved. Meg became pregnant, and after much ado, she and Andy married just days before their daughter Karla was born. A son, David, had joined the family last year. And now there would be another. Considering Andy's schedule and Meg's busy career as an executive at an accounting firm, Will imagined life would be hectic in the Baskin household. He thought they could handle it, however.

Grinning, he stuck out his hand. "Congratulations, pops."

"Yeah, well," Andy said, leaning forward to shake his hand. "I was going to tell you sooner, but with everything else ..." He shrugged.

"I wish you had," Will said with sincerity. "It's nice to hear some good news for a change."

Andy's expression sobered. "Speaking of bad news—what was it you thought Lisa had told me?"

With a dismissive gesture, Will reached for another slice of pizza. "It's nothing."

"Something must have happened. Or else why were you biting my head off a few minutes ago."

"I'm sorry about that."

"Hell, man, things have been tough."

"And about to get tougher." Tight-lipped, Will told Andy about his new assignment and his latest session with the I.A. panel. And though he hadn't intended to spill his guts completely, he ended by detailing his confrontation with Lisa this afternoon. The accusation he had hurled at her sounded even more ridiculous as he repeated it.

But Andy laughed. "I don't know why Lisa got so bent out of shape. Yesterday she was asking me if *I* suspected both of you of something. Like I would ever do that." He shook his head, his mirth disappearing. "Let's face it, this whole situation is making all of us doubt things we never would have questioned in the past."

Will tossed the now unappetizing pizza back into the carton. "And for Lisa and I . . ." He broke off, unable to put his feelings into words.

But Andy had read his mind. "You and Lisa have more at stake than a professional relationship or even friendship."

"You're right." Suddenly restless, Will got to his feet and with hands stuck in his pockets, paced the length of the large open room. He wound up at his piano in the corner. The fine instrument was a twin to the black baby grand at Elena's. Except Will's was covered by a fine layer of dust. He hadn't played it since before Mickey died. Idly, without thought for tune or tempo, he fingered the keys for a moment, then looked at Andy. "I guess I should call Lisa."

Andy shrugged. "That's up to you, of course. But take it from an old hand at avoidance—you're not going to solve anything by hiding out at home with a six-pack for company."

"I know that. It's just—" With a sigh, Will turned back to the piano. He couldn't tell Andy that just looking at Lisa hurt. He didn't want to admit to the cold terror that had gripped him the night Mickey almost killed her. Hurt and terror weren't subjects Will discussed freely, especially with another man, even a friend as close as Andy.

Andy wiped at his mouth with a paper towel, then tossed it aside. "Listen, I didn't come over here to give you advice. I was honestly looking for someone to share the pizza. But since I'm here, I'll say this much. Before this mess, it seemed to me there was something good happening between you and Lisa. I think it would be a shame to let Mickey ruin it for you."

"Ruination seems to have been his specialty."

"Maybe," Andy conceded. "But I still don't get why his failures have to come between you and Lisa."

He made sense, Will admitted grudgingly to himself. He didn't tell Andy that. In fact, he changed the subject altogether and didn't discuss Lisa again before Andy left. But throughout the evening, his friend's words kept prodding him to call Lisa. He must have reached for the phone a dozen times. He even went so far as to plan everything he would say. He wouldn't apologize. He would just act as if nothing had happened. Then they wouldn't have to venture into painful territory.

He took a shower. He got into bed. He gazed at the patch of moonlight on his bedroom ceiling. Finally he picked up the cordless phone beside the bed. And at the sound of Lisa's voice, all his planning was forgotten. His first words were, "I'm sorry."

There was a pause, a shuffling at the other end of the line. "Will?"

He sat up. "Have you got other men calling up to apologize this time of night?"

"No, it's just that the phone has been..." She broke off. "You just startled me, that's all."

"And woke you?"

Her laughter was soft and rueful. "I couldn't sleep."

He plunged ahead with the apology he hadn't intended to make. "I was a jackass this afternoon."

"Jackass isn't quite strong enough to cover what I've been thinking of you all evening."

"I really am sorry."

She sighed. "How could you think that I wouldn't trust you, Will?"

"I didn't really think it, I just..." Frustrated, he raked a hand through his hair. "I guess I just needed to hit out at somebody, and you happened to be a nearby target."

"Oh, Will. Mickey—"

"Don't," he interrupted, his body tensing. "Could we just please have a conversation and leave his name out of it?"

She was a silent a moment, then agreed. "What do you want to talk about?"

"Do you think Elena is doing okay?"

"I think it's too soon after..."

After Mickey's death. The words vibrated across the phone line. Will released a deeply held breath. "Maybe Elena is another subject we should avoid."

"Maybe we should just talk about how much I miss you."

"Miss me?"

"I miss your arms around me."

He smiled into the moonlight. "I've missed that, too."

"Then why aren't we together?"

"I've just been . . ." Will caught himself before the conversation could turn onto a dangerous path. "I don't know, Lisa. I'm not sure what I've been trying to accomplish by staying away from you."

"Then I expect a change, and I expect it soon."

Her soft but firm tones made him chuckle. "Yes, Lieutenant."

"What are you going to do about it?"

Plumping his pillows behind his back, Will settled against the headboard. "How about if I make love to you for a very long time, very soon."

"Talk is cheap, Lieutenant. I hope you know that I expect action."

"Maybe you should tell me exactly what you're going to expect from me, Lieutenant Talbot."

"I think maybe we should start out with a nice, long dinner."

"In bed?"

"Lieutenant!"

"I thought you missed me?"

She laughed, a low, sexy sound that brought an instantaneous response from Will's body. "Maybe we'll make it a nice, short dinner," she amended.

"With dessert in bed?"

"Are you by any chance referring to the infamous strawberry and whipped cream incident that ruined my best sheets?"

The memory elicited a groan from Will. He could see the late September sunshine peeping around the curtains in Lisa's bedroom. And Lisa, all golden skin and mischievous eyes, laughing up at him, her mouth outlined in whipped cream. He had drawn her up to him, licked the cream away, kissed every inch of her. Right now, he could taste the tart berries and the sweet cream and her. The thoughts hardened his body into one long, painful ache.

"Are you still there?" Lisa murmured in his ear.

"I think you need a permit to do this kind of thing over the phone."

"Can't you issue one, Lieutenant?"

"Maybe we should just . . . save it all till we meet."

"And when will that be?"

"Tomorrow? We'll go to dinner."

"It's Saturday, so make it lunch. Afterward, I'll send Terry somewhere for the afternoon."

"Sending your child away?"

"He needs a happy mother."

"You sound eager."

"I hope you are."

He laughed, shifted slightly to alleviate the ache in his groin. "You have no idea how eager—"

"Oh, but I do," Lisa murmured. "I do know. That's why *I'm* so eager." Still laughing, she clicked off the phone.

Blindly, Will flipped the cordless phone's button and flung it aside. He smiled and stretched, his thoughts filled with memories of Lisa, his body pulsing for the release he would find in her body.

It was more than physical, of course. She aroused him on so many levels. With her quick mind. Her sense of humor. Her caring nature. At thirty-four, Will had known his share of women, but none of them had complemented him in the way that Lisa did. She was older than him by a few years. She had known heartbreak and loss. She was the most exciting woman he had ever known.

Will chuckled. Some of the women in his past would probably think it ironic how entangled he was with Lisa. Until her, he had tended to avoid relationships with women who had children. A psychologist would most likely suggest it had something to do with his own fatherless childhood. Perhaps, as one woman had bitterly suggested, he knew children would demand a complete involvement from him. She had been right, of course. Children did make demands. Only when it came to Lisa and Terry, Will hadn't cared about the demands. In fact, he welcomed them.

Even before the August night he and Lisa had become lovers, his life was irrevocably meshed with hers. It had started the moment they met. Something in her self-assured manner had both bothered and attracted him. She had called him cocky and self-involved, but had seemed to enjoy their arguments. Then he discovered how smart she was, found out how respected she was in the department. Then their friendship had begun.

Only friendship? He had told himself and everyone else they were friends. But he could remember almost three years ago, standing at a party, getting steamed as he'd watched some older guy flirt with her. She had been flirting back, but Will had wanted to warn the guy off. He'd told himself it was because he liked her and didn't like the guy. He'd pretended his feelings were brotherly, even though she aroused some distinctly unsiblinglike responses. He'd spent half the night thinking about Lisa Talbot.

She was shot the next day.

Will sobered, thinking of the long hours he had spent at the hospital, waiting for Lisa to pull through surgery and its aftermath. Before then, he hadn't prayed in a long time. It wasn't that he was completely without religion; Elena had made sure he'd received a solid grounding in their faith. But as a young man, he had decided your actions counted a whole lot more than the time you spent on your knees or the number of candles you lit. While Lisa hung between life and death, however, he had sent some earnest pleas heavenward. They had been answered. She had survived.

Then Will followed the answered prayer up with some action. Lisa had no family, so she had needed him, needed all her friends after the shooting. She had the stress of going back on the job after a near-death incident, and the added strain of convincing Terry that she wouldn't be hurt again.

But she had been hurt.

She had almost died.

Groaning, Will buried his face in his hands. It always came back to this. He could dream of warm, sweet afternoons in Lisa's arms, but nothing could ever erase the fact that Mickey had tried to kill her. For the rest of Will's life, he would remember the moment Mickey had held Lisa's life out like some bargaining chip in a poker game.

Choose. It's me or her. Your choice, Will, he'd said.

Will flung back the sheets, grabbed his robe and stalked into the living room. As if that could turn his thoughts from their treacherous path. As if anything he could ever do would make that terrible night disappear.

Your choice, Will.

Could he have killed Mickey? Will hadn't dared ask himself that question until now. But if events had proceeded differently, he might have been forced to take Mickey out. There was no question that it would have been the right choice. But could Will have done it? If worse had come to worst, could he have saved Lisa by killing Mickey?

There had been other moments in Will's career when he had faced hard choices. He had been in tight spots. But in thirteen years on the force, the questions of right or wrong and life or death had never been as clear cut as on that cold November night. He had always been certain then that when presented with such a choice, he would do what was right, without hesitation, without thought.

But he wondered now. Could he have pulled that trigger? Even though it was right. Even though it would have saved Lisa.

Lisa. His hot, sensual thoughts of her were gone, replaced by self-doubt and conjecture. He wanted to believe he would have been her hero, if need be. But he couldn't be sure. He would never be sure.

As if drawn by a magnet, Will's gaze slipped to the pictures grouped on the wall behind the piano. Their glass gleamed in the moonlight, beckoned him closer. In the center was a framed snapshot of himself and Mickey, taken on the day Will had graduated from the police academy. Mickey's arm was flung around his shoulders; his smile was so proud. On that day, Will had been so sure of himself. And why not? Mickey had taught him everything he needed to know about life. That day, he had stepped in line with his uncle in a fight for what was good and honest and just.

The picture was a lie, however. Everything Mickey had professed to stand for was a lie.

The truth was years of big and little deceptions.

The truth was betrayal.

The truth was the moment he had stuck that gun in Lisa's face.

Muttering an oath, Will ripped the picture from the wall. He tore down every picture of Mickey. He threw them all in the fireplace. Then he struck a match and watched them burn.

But when they were ashes, his anger still smoldered.

Chapter Four

Saturday didn't begin the way Lisa had planned.

She did her part. Champagne was in readiness in the refrigerator. Her most naughty teddy was beneath her jeans and sweatshirt. She'd even made arrangements for Terry to go to the park with Andy, Meg and their children after lunch.

But she knew the minute Will appeared at her door that her plans were going awry.

He looked terrible—his face gaunt and pale, his eyes with the haunted look she was beginning to dread. She knew the last thing he wanted or needed was a series of questions on how he felt or what had changed since last evening's sensual exchange on the telephone.

So she just tried to act as if nothing was wrong. As she had done a hundred times, she greeted him with a kiss. She told herself it didn't matter that he didn't kiss

her back. She sent him out into the backyard to pass a
football around with Terry while she finished preparing lunch. Silently she kept repeating, *He needs time.
An important component of his life is gone. I have to
be patient and understanding.*

But as she stood by the window, watching a grim-faced Will toss the ball to her oddly quiet son, she
wondered how far patience and understanding would
stretch.

The phone rang, jarring her from her thoughts, but
the caller clicked off when she answered. "Damn," she
muttered, slamming down the receiver. Two other
hang-ups had occurred last night before Will called.
Her annoyance was giving way to anger. If someone
who had been involved with Mickey thought they could
harass or intimidate her with those kinds of tactics,
they were way off base. Smothering her irritation, she
called Terry and Will in to lunch.

While Will went to freshen up in the bathroom,
Terry scrubbed his hands at the kitchen sink. The boy's
usual stream of chatter was missing.

Lisa set a pitcher of iced tea on the kitchen table.
"Something bothering you, son?"

"No." His monotone said yes.

"You sure?"

Frowning, he dried his hands on the towel she passed
him. "I think Will's mad about something."

She stifled a sigh, and spoke quietly. "Didn't we already talk about this? I told you Will might not be the
same for a while."

"I know. I know. I just didn't know he would be sad
for so long."

"It hasn't been long," Lisa said, though she was sympathetic. Nine days could seem like centuries when you were a youngster.

"Is everyone always this sad when someone dies?"

"Yes, they are. Now give Will a break, okay?" She turned from the sink to find Will in the kitchen doorway. His expression told her he had heard most of her exchange with Terry. She didn't try to offer any explanations, just picked up a basket of rolls and said, "I hope you're hungry. I've been slaving in the kitchen since early morning."

Will's smile looked just as artificial as hers felt, but he put forth an effort to be sociable during lunch. He had seconds of the grilled chicken and Lisa's special homemade potato salad. He talked to her about everyday matters—a leak in her roof, the most recent world crises, a movie they had seen several weeks ago. And he tried teasing Terry—about the boy's favorite football team's lousy record, about asking Lisa for a snake for Christmas, about a girl who had sent him a love letter in class.

But her son wasn't buying Will's act. He refused to be drawn out, picked at his food and regarded both adults with wariness. Will finally stopped trying. Lisa felt her forced cheerfulness begin to slip, also. Their somber mood was in sharp contrast to the boisterous meals the three of them had shared in the past. By the time she served cream-cheese cherry pie for dessert, her nerves were stretched thin, like a balloon that had been inflated and deflated too many times.

"Aren't you going to eat?" she asked Terry when he sat staring at his pie. "It's your favorite."

"And it's delicious," Will offered. "Thanks for making it, Lisa."

Terry obediently lifted his fork, then looked at Lisa. "Is my dad dead?"

She felt her mouth drop open, but recovered as fast as she could. "Of course not. Why would you ask such a thing?"

"Since dying makes everybody so sad, I thought maybe he was dead and you just didn't want to make me feel bad."

Lisa spared a glance at Will, who had set down his fork and was looking at Terry with an unreadable expression on his face. "Your father isn't dead," she said firmly. "He sends money every month to help me take care of you. He lives far away. In Oregon."

"Kevin's dad lives in California, and Kevin goes to see him. On the map in geography class, Oregon isn't very far from California. Why can't I see my dad?"

He hadn't asked these questions in a long time, so they caught Lisa off guard. He was getting older, too, and she knew the simple answers and evasions she used to give him wouldn't suffice now. Yet he seemed too young to hear the truth—that his father didn't want to see him. She drew in a breath and tried to formulate a reply.

But Will cut in. "Different kids have different kinds of fathers, Terry. Yours just can't see you. But he does make sure you're taken care of. That's why he sends your mother money, to buy you clothes and toys and stuff."

Lisa sent him a grateful glance. It sounded like a good answer.

Terry, however, still looked skeptical. "Have you ever met him?"

"No," Will replied. "But I believe what your mother tells me about him."

The boy's eyes narrowed. "She told me Santa Claus was real, too, and that was a lie."

No wonder some child psychologists thought that particular fantasy could backfire, she thought. Then she attempted another explanation. "Terry, your father—"

"How do I know you're not lying about him?" Two spots of color, always an indication of his agitation, appeared in his cheeks. "I think he's lost or dead or something, and you just won't tell me."

"I don't lie to you about your father," Lisa said with quiet authority. "Now either eat your dessert or go to your room and wait for Andy and Meg to come by."

He flung his fork down. "I'm not going with them. Their kids are babies. They don't want me with them."

"That's not true. They asked you to go to the park."

"That's a lie, too," Terry said, clearly angry now. "I heard you on the phone asking if I could go with them."

Will spoke up again. "Son, if you're mad at me—"

"I'm not your son and I'm not mad at you!" He stormed from the room. A few seconds later a door slammed upstairs.

Will pushed away from the table. "I'll go talk to him."

"No."

"But he's upset, and it's my fault."

Elbows on the table, Lisa rested her chin on her steepled fingers. "He's too emotional right now. It's best to leave him alone for a while."

"I hope you didn't mind my butting in."

"Why would I mind? You're a part of his life. If I had ever had any objection to you disciplining him, or talking to him about anything, you would have heard it before now. I actually appreciated your attempt to help."

Will rubbed his forehead as if it ached. "I'm sorry I upset him."

"Did something happen outside?"

"I guess I just wasn't really paying attention to him. My mind's on other things."

"Well, you've spoiled him rotten in the past. You guys are buddy-buddy most of the time. Even when you and I are going out without him, you always pay special attention to him. I'm afraid he's gotten used to it."

"And now I'm preoccupied," Will said with a sigh. "I just didn't feel much like joking around with him earlier."

"He has to learn that the universe isn't his to command."

"I think he knows that. If he could command anything, his father would want to see him." Will sat forward, his dark eyes concerned. "Maybe you should call Rich Talbot, tell him what a great kid his son is, tell him how much Terry wants to know him."

She stiffened at the suggestion. "I gave Rich every opportunity to be a part of Terry's life. He prefers to ease his conscience with a check every month. I'm not going to beg him to change now. Especially when I know how selfish he is. Terry doesn't need him."

Will shook his head. "That's not true. Rich may not be the kind of father he should be, but that doesn't mean Terry doesn't need him."

"I think a bad father is worse than none at all," she insisted. "And it's not as if Terry has no male influences in his life. There's you and Andy, teachers, his Little League coaches—"

"But none of us is his father."

"That doesn't matter. What matters is the time and attention you give him. I've been grateful that you guys seem to enjoy being with him, that he enjoys you."

Will shoved a hand through his hair, his mouth set in a rueful line. "Yeah, I've given him lots of great time and attention today, haven't I?"

She touched his arm. "I can assure you that one or two bad days aren't going to scar him for life."

Frowning, Will looked out the window. "Maybe we should all go to the park together this afternoon. Maybe part of the reason Terry is upset is because he felt we were pushing him away."

It wasn't the day Lisa had envisioned, but there were worse suggestions than spending a crisp Georgia-perfect November afternoon with Will and her son. After all, Will could just go home, and Terry could spend the rest of the day up in his room. That would be much worse.

Seizing on the idea of a family-type outing, Lisa called Meg and Andy and arranged to meet them at the park. Terry sulked for a while in the car, but by the time they arrived at Piedmont Park, he was his usual sunny self. Lisa supposed a stricter mother might have made him apologize to Will for his outburst, but she thought it best to leave the situation alone. Besides, there was nothing really wrong between Will and Terry. She set her worries aside and determined to enjoy the day.

Her surroundings made that easy. Piedmont Park was Atlanta's outdoor recreation center, a haven for joggers, bikers and tennis enthusiasts. On a Saturday afternoon such as this, even with a full lineup of college football games on the tube, the area was packed. But they managed to find an unbroken stretch of grass where Lisa joined the guys for a game of touch football. Meg cheered them on and tended her children from a nearby picnic blanket, while Andy's aging Irish setter, Boomer, stood guard over them all.

The game was played hard. Will seemed determined to shake off the gloom that had dogged him all day. He threw himself into the competition—insulting Andy's abilities, encouraging Terry's, pretending to be astounded at Lisa's. She had been a good athlete in high school and college, and kept in shape now by running and swimming whenever she had the chance. It was fun to pit her speed and agility against the men's, to elude them whenever she could. And it was just as much fun to allow Will to catch her, to swing her around, to hold her just a few minutes more than necessary.

Once he surprised her from the side and pulled her close for a brief but hard kiss. Will looked sheepish, but she was so startled, she dropped the ball. He yelled

"Fumble," recovered the ball and raced away from her for a touchdown.

"No fair," Andy protested. "Kissing is not an acceptable defensive maneuver."

Grinning, Will tossed him the ball. "It depends on who you kiss, *amigo.*" Puckering his lips, he started after Andy. While Terry rolled in the grass laughing and Lisa waited for them to recover their dignity, the two men chased each other around like young boys. Boomer, roused from his afternoon nap, joined in the melee, barking and nipping at his master's heels. Finally, worn out, the three adult players flopped to the ground near Meg and the children. Terry and Boomer continued running in circles.

Andy had fallen in a heap, declaring he would never rise again. He closed his eyes and pretended to sleep. But Will was attacked by nearly-three-year-old Karla, who threw herself on him, declaring, "Silly, Will, you don't kiss Daddy."

"Oh, yeah?" he asked, tickling her sides. "Then I'll just have to kiss you, won't I?" They laughed and tickled and cuddled until her eleven-month-old brother toddled over to get in on the action.

Several yards away, Lisa sat transfixed. The sight of Will romping with these two dark-haired youngsters brought a lump to her throat. An unexpected yearning filled her chest. She hadn't felt this way in a long time, not since she had decided to have Terry. She could clearly remember the time when her arms had ached to hold her own child, when just the sight of a baby could bring tears to her eyes. Those feelings, dormant for years, were coursing through her again.

Over the children's heads, Will looked up and caught her gaze. They shared a long, lingering glance. And for a moment Lisa allowed herself to fantasize about having a baby with him. A girl, she decided dreamily. A sister for Terry. With Will's dark hair and black eyes...

A low voice interrupted the daydream. "My, my, but I recognize that look."

Lisa turned, met Meg's knowing glance, but pretended innocence. "What look?"

Meg spoke quietly, for Lisa's ears only. "There's something about a big, strong man and a little child that does us in, isn't there?"

Conceding defeat, Lisa nodded. Then she directed a sly glance toward her friend's stomach. "Is that what keeps happening to you with Andy?"

Meg's gleaming dark hair swung forward as she smiled. "He and I just have this incredibly bad luck with birth control."

"You don't look too unhappy about the situation."

"I'm not," Meg replied. "But we won't have to worry about this happening again. With three kids under four, Andy and I will never have time to make another one."

Lisa laughed and settled back, her gaze drawn once again to Will and the children.

Meg was silent for a moment, then said softly, "How is he? I mean, he seems okay right now, but Andy told me he's not coping very well."

"No, he's not."

"And what about you?"

"I'm just trying to be there for him."

"I meant, how are you handling the situation?"

Lisa glanced up, confused.

"Not with Will," Meg explained. "With yourself. You went through a terrible ordeal, Lisa. I hope you're giving yourself time to recover."

"I stay busy."

"Too busy to sleep?"

Frowning, Lisa shrugged.

"You and Will both look as if you haven't had a decent night's rest since this happened."

"I guess I haven't," Lisa admitted. "I wouldn't know about Will, of course. He's stayed at Elena's quite a bit and..."

"Generally avoided being alone with you," Meg completed for her. "And you need him."

Lisa broke off a blade of grass and shredded it between her fingers. "I think he's the one with the most needs right now."

"Are you sure about that?"

"I'm doing fine," Lisa insisted. "Sure, I've had some bad dreams about that night. Sometimes the whole incident gets tangled up with when I was shot before. But I'm coping. With a little time, when all our names are cleared, when Will gets beyond all this, then everything will go back to the way it was before Mickey died."

Meg's dark eyes narrowed with concern. "Just don't hide your feelings from him, Lisa. Don't pretend that everything is okay with you if it isn't. Sometimes I think you cops take an oath to bury your true emotions. But stoicism isn't bravery. Very often it takes more courage to face your feelings than to pretend they don't exist."

"Spoken like a true cop's mate," Lisa said, smiling slightly.

"I don't mean to preach." Meg reached out and squeezed Lisa's arm. "I just want you and Will to make it through this with your relationship intact."

Lisa patted her hand and pretended an assurance she didn't feel. "We will."

"And maybe soon we'll be going to a wedding." Meg's impish grin flashed as she stood and went toward her children. "Will," she called. "Don't you know my son isn't supposed to eat dirt?"

A wedding. Smiling, Lisa turned her face up to the clear blue sky and drew in the fresh scents of earth and grass. She closed her eyes and let the peacefulness of the afternoon envelope her. Meg was so funny. No doubt she had Lisa and Will's wedding planned, even though Lisa had never considered marriage. She wanted Will in her life, yes. And given the strength of the yearning that had gone through her a little while ago, she might consider bearing his child. But marriage? Her only experience with the institution hadn't been good.

Besides, she and Will had a long way to go before they could think about their future. They both needed to pull themselves together.

She opened her eyes to find Will standing over her. He grinned and offered her his hand. "Come on, lazy bones, let's go for a walk."

"I'm too exhausted."

"Come on." He leaned down and pulled her to her feet.

They didn't move, however. Her hand remained in his. Their eyes were nearly level, their gazes locked. Lisa's thoughts were on the way he had kissed her earlier, their only real kiss in weeks. She wanted to kiss him now. But what she wanted more was to move beyond this terrible hesitation. There was no reason not to kiss him. So she did.

As he had been doing all afternoon, Will just went with the moment. He concentrated on sensations. The softness of Lisa's mouth. The instantaneous desire that licked through his gut. He told himself the here and now was all that mattered.

She drew away and smiled. A radiant, purely Lisa smile. And she didn't say anything. She knew, just as he did, that words weren't necessary. She just took his hand, and they walked toward the path where Terry was waiting with the Irish setter.

For the first time in days, Will took real notice of the world around him. He took pleasure in the sound of Terry's laugh, the warmth of the sun on his shoulders. The ache inside him eased somewhat. Another golden, precious hour passed in which he wasn't consumed by anger or guilt, or any negative emotion. The day, which had started so badly, had turned into perfection.

Everyone seemed reluctant to leave. But Andy and Meg had two sleepy children to take home, and even Terry's boundless energy was flagging. The lengthening shadows and cooler air forced them to call it a day. With a folded blanket in one hand and the other on the boy's shoulder, Will led their small procession to the parking lot.

And came face-to-face with a fellow officer.

The man wasn't dressed for duty. In fact, he had his wife and daughter with him. But Will couldn't miss the look in his eyes. The measuring glance that he passed over all of them. The way he turned his head, as if he hoped they hadn't seen him.

Will knew he would never grow used to seeing such doubt in another cop's gaze. He'd be damned if he was going to let this man walk past him without an acknowledgment. "Washington," he said, thrusting his hand out. "It looks like you've been enjoying the mild weather, too."

The man looked at his hand for minute, but he did grasp it. He had a strong grip. Will had always regarded him as a good man. He shook hands with Andy and Lisa, too. Children and wives were introduced.

And then all of them stood there. Unmoving. Awkward. Will's morning headache began to pound again. He felt his muscles tense as he waited for Washington to say something he could challenge.

He didn't, however. Someone—Meg, maybe—got them all started toward the cars again. But as the other officer and his family walked away, Will heard the wife whisper, "That was them, right?" Washington shushed her, but the damage was already done.

Lisa caught Will's arm before he could react. He didn't know what he had intended to do, but she stopped him with a gentle, "Let it go."

He did. But the day was tarnished beyond repair. He took Lisa and Terry home and turned down their invitations to stay.

Lisa rebuked him with her wide, blue eyes. "That guy's not worth getting upset over."

Will shrugged. And then he left.

He hurt too much to be with her, to be with anyone tonight. Today he had put some stitches in the wounds inside him. Now they were ripped, and he was bleeding again.

Hurting this way made him feel weak and out of control. He wanted to be unaffected by the opinions of others. But, damn it, it mattered. His honor was being questioned. And for as long as Will could remember, he had been taught a man's honor and reputation were as important as his life.

But what could he do about it? Even when the I.A. cleared his name, he knew the doubts would linger with some people. It should be enough to know he hadn't done anything wrong. But the lingering notion that he hadn't done enough, that he should have known what Mickey was really doing, overshadowed everything else.

There was only one solution. He had to prove himself. Monday, he was starting a new job. Monday, he was going to redeem the family honor. No matter what it took, he would put an end to the rumors and doubt.

He carried that resolve through the night and the next day, all the way till Monday morning.

Then he had to walk into a crowded squad room. He purposely got there just before the shift briefing and roll call. He wanted to meet them all at once, wanted to gauge their reaction to him. There were familiar faces in the group. The field training officer was a woman he had worked with in the past. The sergeant had a good reputation. There were others with whom he had conferred when he was working in Homicide.

And among those faces, he found some that gave him welcome, some that studied him with cautious eyes. He knew most of them had to have heard the rumors by now. He wondered who believed what.

As a lieutenant on patrol, Will wasn't assigned a partner. His job was to be one of two supervisory personnel for the first shift in a specified district. So, technically, many of these people would be under his command. His boss was a thirty year veteran who asked Will to stay after everyone else had rolled out on patrol. Leaning against a wall to the side of the room, Will waited for the man to have his say.

Captain Marshall perched on the edge of a desk and gave Will a long, hard look. "Are you sure you want to be here?" he asked after a few moments had passed.

"This is my new assignment."

"You could have taken some time off. You've been through a lot." Neither his voice nor his expression betrayed what he thought of what Will had been through.

Will straightened away from the wall. "I'd rather work, Captain."

"Okay," Marshall said, shrugging. "The other lieutenant on the shift has off days on Sunday and Monday. You'll meet him tomorrow. The two of you need to cooperate, so make an effort. The sergeant and master patrolman are good officers, too. Ask them for anything you need. This is a top-flight group."

"Yes, sir. I'm glad to be here."

Marshall's smile said he doubted that, but he didn't make a comment. "I understand you know the area fairly well?"

"I worked here before, sir. On the Narcotics Task Force."

"And you did good work there, I understand."

"Yes, sir, I did."

"Well, you know procedure. You know where your car is. Let me know if there's something you need."

"Yes, sir." Will went to the doorway, then turned back. "There's just one thing I want to make clear, Captain Marshall."

The man looked up from the papers in his hand. "What's that?"

"If somebody gets their butt in a sling out there, I'm on the right side."

One of Marshall's eyebrows raised. "Did I imply that you wouldn't be?"

"I'm just making my position clear."

"Good. You do your job and keep your nose clean, and we'll all be happy." He looked back at the papers, and Will knew he had been dismissed.

He walked to his assigned squad car, cursing himself. He didn't need to explain himself. Why had he bothered? He just felt so damn out of kilter.

A little later, however, as he sent his car speeding through the cool early morning, he began to relax. The resolve that had fired him over the weekend began to return. The car radio crackled, calling out the code for a holdup in progress a few blocks away. Will radioed a response and headed toward the holdup. A familiar rush of adrenaline shot through him. This was home. Here, he could prove himself again.

Someone was watching.

The knowledge jerked Lisa from a deep sleep. For

several minutes she lay in the darkness, breathing hard, perspiration pooling under her neck and between her breasts. It took that long for her to realize she had been dreaming. She and Will had been in a room, a hospital room, she thought. He had been in bed, lying still and silent while she stood next to him. And she had known someone else was watching them.

The dream's meaning was crystal clear.

Taking a deep breath, she reached for the lamp beside her bed. Thunder shook the house before she could flip the switch, however, startling her. Lightning flashed through the room. Now she knew the real reason she had awakened. They were paying for several days of unseasonably mild weather with a storm. She turned on her lamp just as the first drops of rain hit against the windows.

She groaned, thinking of the leak in the ceiling of the upstairs guest room. Not bothering with her robe, she went to the kitchen for a bucket and then climbed the stairs. No water had appeared as yet, but the stain on the ceiling showed where it could be expected. She put the bucket in place, then tiptoed into Terry's room to make sure the storm hadn't disturbed him.

He slept with one arm and a leg stuck out from under his blankets. Thunder cracked again, and he didn't stir. Lisa drew the covers over him and went back downstairs.

She was too hyper to sleep. In three hours she would have to get up and go to work, anyway. Her new assignment was in old territory. She had gone back to arson investigations, the area she had specialized in before being drawn into Internal Affairs. Today, her first day back, all she had done was familiarize herself with the cases now under investigation. The people she was working with were familiar for the most part. Nothing had been said about Mickey or Will. Everyone had seemed determined to just do the job. That suited Lisa fine.

She wondered how Will was making out.

She hadn't heard from him since Saturday. She had called him, leaving messages on his machine that he hadn't bothered to answer. He might be at Elena's, she knew, but she stopped short of phoning him there. He knew where to find her. Elena had called her, however, with an invitation for Lisa and Terry to join her for Thanksgiving dinner on Thursday. There was no way Lisa could refuse the woman, but she wondered if Will would welcome her presence. Every time they seemed to be on the brink of reestablishing their old ease with one another, something or someone came between them. Lisa knew she had to find a way to bring them together. What it would be, she hadn't a clue.

Thunder rolled overhead, a fainter sound this time, and Lisa shivered. The storm had sent temperatures plunging. Rubbing arms left bare by her sleeveless nightgown, she went to check her heating unit. She reset the thermostat and turned out the living room lights. The rain was really coming down, blowing across the front porch and hitting the living room windows. She pushed aside the curtains to check, but as was the way of thunderstorms, the rain abated suddenly. It still fell, just not in wind-driven sheets. She was about to let the curtains drop into place when she saw a car parked across the street.

Moving to the side of the window, she peered out again. Though the car was sitting near a streetlight, she couldn't make out the color, couldn't tell if it was occupied. There were no houses across the street, only a small, central, neighborhood park. It was more like an empty lot, really, which all the homeowners on her circle helped to maintain. The kids liked to use it for their games. Some of the gardeners in the community planted flowers there every spring. But no one usually parked there.

"Which doesn't mean they couldn't tonight," Lisa muttered to herself. It was a holiday week. For all she knew, one of her neighbors had out-of-town guests and needed extra parking space.

Even as she told herself to be sensible, Lisa thought of Andy's suspicions. She thought of the hang-up calls. Perhaps she should call and have a squad car drive by and check this out. She moved toward the phone, then caught herself. The last thing she wanted was for everyone to know Lisa Talbot was having patrolmen check out cars parked beside empty lots on public streets. She could check it out herself, of course.

"And get soaked for nothing," she murmured.

No, she was just being paranoid. There was no reason to worry about a car.

Nevertheless, she double-checked doors and windows and her burglar alarm. And she peeked out the window once more. The car hadn't moved.

She made herself go to bed. She closed her eyes, counted to one hundred. But just as her body relaxed, she remembered her dream.

Someone was watching.

That thought kept her awake until exhaustion took over.

Chapter Five

The car was gone the next morning.

Lisa stared out the window to the spot where it had been parked and wondered if the whole episode had been part of her dream. But the water in the bucket in the guest bedroom proved she had been awakened from the storm, and her dull, throbbing headache gave testimony to her sleepless hours. Her fears seemed foolish, however, when examined in the gray, foggy daylight.

She didn't have time to worry about it this morning, not with the usual bustle of getting herself and Terry off to work and school. She was running behind schedule just enough to catch the worst of the early morning traffic. As a result, she walked into the office a few minutes late and found a department meeting already in progress. For a second all eyes were on her.

"Sorry," she mumbled as she set her purse down on her desk.

The captain who headed up the arson department, a man Lisa hadn't worked with before, nodded at her. "We meet fifteen minutes every Tuesday morning to go over the current cases. I guess that's a new policy since you left the department. I thought I had told you."

He hadn't, but Lisa didn't make it an issue. She just dragged her chair to the center of the room and joined the department's other three officers. She couldn't bear to think anyone would withhold such petty information in order to make her look bad. That kind of paranoia was what had caused last night's dream and her terror over an innocently parked car. Telling herself to get a grip, she concentrated on the list of cases the captain was going through.

Many people assumed arson investigations were conducted only by the fire department. But once arson had been confirmed, the police department was called in on the case. Some policemen liked to say that firemen carried children out of fiery blazes and rescued cats from trees, while the police were left to hand out citations and arrest the arsonists.

Burning buildings and vehicles were often used to commit murder or to cover up evidence of that crime and many others. It was while working on just such a case that Lisa had been shot. A developer had torched a newly constructed building to rid himself of an unwanted partner. The death had looked like an accident, but Lisa had been suspicious. One of the developer's employees had been, too, and had agreed to wear a wire in an attempt to elicit a confession from the man. But the developer sensed something was up, pulled out a gun, and when Lisa moved in to try to protect the employee, she was shot.

Nothing so dramatic was included in the department's present caseload, but that changed when the captain took a phone call to end their meeting.

Hanging up, he turned to Lisa. "They've found a body in a burning car over on the west side. Go take a look."

The crime scene was ghastly. Hours after she had left the gory details to the crime lab technicians, Lisa carried the horrid smell of smoke and death with her. In her hair. On her clothes. She couldn't wait to get home so she could scrub the stench away, but there was paperwork to be done and calls to be made before she could leave. When she emerged from headquarters into the early winter twilight, Will was waiting in the parking lot, and she forgot about the horror she had witnessed today.

He didn't see her right away, and she paused a short distance away to study him. He leaned against the driver's door of her blue Bronco, the brim of his uniform hat pulled low on his forehead, his arms folded across his chest. The weather had indeed turned colder since last night's storm, but his short jacket, navy blue like his uniform, was unbuttoned against the chill. Black leather gloves were sticking out of one pocket. The cold had put color in his cheeks. His dark hair curled just above his collar in the back. Lisa thought he could have posed for a police recruiting poster. Women, at least, would be signing up in record numbers.

"It's a good thing I'm immune to the charms of a man in uniform," she said as she came closer. "Otherwise, I might disgrace us both right now."

Will looked up and despite himself had to smile at Lisa. Who could help but return a smile like hers? She looked tired and pale, but her smile had enough energy to light up the city. Grinning, he pulled off his hat as she approached.

She stopped at his side. "I was hoping to hear from you today. Did you get my messages?"

"I've been busy," he lied. Though he had been spending a lot of time trying to sort through Elena's financial affairs, he hadn't been so busy he couldn't have called Lisa. He had told himself to stay away from her and Andy, that their relationship with him had caused them enough problems. But today he had found an excuse to see her.

"You want to go somewhere to talk or just stand out here?"

"This is fine if you're not too cold."

Her breath formed a cloud as she spoke. "It feels good to me. Maybe the cold snap will make it seem more like the holiday season."

"That's what I wanted to talk to you about," Will said. "You're going to Elena's for Thanksgiving dinner, aren't you?"

Lisa hesitated, her expression unsure as she looked at him. "I told her I would. Do you want me to stay away?"

"Of course not," he retorted, his tone harsher than he intended. He cleared his throat before continuing.

"It's just that she got the idea you didn't really want to come."

"I did wonder how you would feel about it. We hadn't talked since Saturday, and I just . . ." Her voice trailed away as she shrugged.

He dragged a hand through his hair. "I really am sorry I haven't been able to call."

She lifted her chin and dismissed the apology with a wave of her hand. "It's okay. I know you've been busy, getting back to work and all. And like I said, I was planning to be at Elena's on Thursday. I didn't realize I hadn't made that clear to her, but I'll call her tonight and make sure she doesn't give it another minute's worry. This will be our third Thanksgiving at her house. Terry's already looking forward to Marta's pumpkin pie."

"He'll make the day easier for Elena," Will said with a sigh. "Everything is so different for her this year."

"For you, too."

"Yeah, well . . ." He looked away. "I need to get rolling, I guess."

Lisa glanced at her watch. "I do, too. Terry has to be picked up at the Y by seven."

Will seized upon Terry as a relatively safe subject. "How did his basketball tryout go yesterday?"

"He made first string."

"Hey, that's great. Tell him I'm proud."

"Why don't you tell him yourself? Come have dinner with us. It'll probably be take-out chicken, but—"

"I really can't," Will cut in.

Disappointment glimmered for a moment in Lisa's eyes, but she covered it well, reaching into her purse to get her keys. "I guess I'm lucky to have seen you at all."

Ignoring the faint edge of sarcasm in her voice, he straightened himself up from the car and put his hat back on. "I just wanted to ask you about Thursday, and since I had to come to headquarters anyway, I waited for you."

Lisa glanced up, sarcasm gone. "They didn't call you in for more questions, did they?"

"No." He tugged at the brim of his hat, not bothering to hide his irritation. "I had to deliver some paperwork for my shift supervisor. It seems he's decided I'm going to be a messenger boy."

"It's that bad, huh?"

He moved his shoulders carelessly. "It's all right, I guess. Except that all day today, the captain has been riding with one of the other officers. They keep showing up at the calls I'm on. I feel like he's looking over my shoulder."

"Pretty soon he'll figure out he's just wasting his time."

"Maybe. He's not the only problem, though. This morning I met the shift's resident loudmouth jerk."

"There's one of those on every shift."

"Yes, well, this one happens to be the other lieutenant."

"That could be unpleasant."

"I hope not. I'm just going to stay clear of him as much as I can." Will didn't elaborate on the way the man had sat across the room during roll call, his lip curled as he stared at Will, his eyes full of challenge. He didn't want Lisa to know how badly he had wanted to knock the guy's teeth down his throat. "How about you?" he asked. "Work going okay?"

"Oh, the usual stuff," she said. "Burning bodies in cars."

Will studied her pale features closely. "You want to talk about it?"

She shook her head. "It's nothing I can't handle. I'm just glad to be back at work, aren't you?"

He said yes, but it wasn't really the truth. After two days on his new assignment, his plans for proving himself seemed pretty foolish. He had felt the familiar excitement in responding to a call, had taken the usual satisfaction from helping someone in trouble. But most of the time he felt as if he was moving in slow motion, just doing the job. His work had never felt like just a job before.

Mickey had taught him that being a cop was too important to be only a means to a paycheck. From the beginning of his career, Will had approached each assignment with enthusiasm. What he did hadn't always been pleasant. But his positive attitude had carried him through. Now that zeal had been profoundly altered. He questioned it, as he questioned everything his uncle had taught him. He felt as if his entire life was skewed, out of focus.

And he didn't quite understand why his off-balance sensation was at its worst when he was with Lisa. There was more to it than looking at her and remembering Mickey's attempt on her life. Maybe it was because he knew Lisa wouldn't allow him to pretend. What he wanted most was to forget everything that had happened, wipe Mickey from his life, bury the pain. But

Lisa would never let him take that route. She was too direct for such self-deception, and she wouldn't tolerate it from him.

He used to like that directness. Lisa had never employed the coy evasions he had disliked in so many other women. He knew where he stood with her at all times. Even when she flirted, she was straightforward. Small talk wasn't her thing. And that was the problem he faced with her now. At this point in time, he didn't want the open, honest communication they had shared in the past. He wanted to pretend, to hide, to evade.

In essence, the very qualities that had drawn him to Lisa now pushed him away.

While he pondered that realization, she glanced at her watch again. "I really have to go. You're sure you can't come over?"

"Sorry."

"Another time, then."

He thought they sounded like casual friends rather than lovers. Only maybe they weren't really lovers anymore. As lovers they had been in sync. Now they were like the hands of a broken clock, moving in opposite directions. They crossed, but never connected. The knowledge troubled him, but he knew it was probably for the best. He couldn't handle Lisa right now, couldn't answer the questions he knew she wanted to ask, couldn't drag his feelings out for her to analyze.

She unlocked her car door, got in and bestowed her bright, perfect smile on him again. "I'll see you Thanksgiving."

He nodded, closed the door and stood watching until her Bronco's red taillights had blended with the rest of the early evening traffic.

Thanksgiving. The very thought of the holiday made Will shiver. He didn't know how Elena was going to get through it. She had been very emotional the past few days, and he had suggested they forego a holiday celebration this year. Some friends of hers from the church had asked her to join their family for lunch, but she had refused. She had insisted on planning a big meal and inviting Lisa and Terry. And if that was the way she wanted it, Will was determined to make the day as normal as possible.

As the hours ticked away, however, bringing the event closer, his dread grew.

Thanksgiving had always been Mickey's favorite day. He had told Will he'd inherited his love of the holiday from his immigrant father, a man who had overflowed with pride in his adopted country. In the early days of Mickey and Elena's marriage, he had often worked on Thanksgiving, so they had established the custom of a dinner rather than a midday meal. Many officers had been known to eat lunch with their families, then go to Mickey's for their second helpings and dessert. There were always two or three tables full of guests, and Marta always ran around just before the food was served, setting places for last-minute arrivals Mickey had forgotten to tell her about.

Mickey had always selected the turkey, even before Elena's illness forced her to leave the marketing to others. He'd always chopped the celery for the dressing. He'd always whipped the potatoes and made rich, brown gravy. And he'd always said the same special blessing before carving the bird.

But what Mickey had always done was no more.

After he came off duty on Thanksgiving afternoon, Will steeled himself not to compare this day to those in the past. He tried not to think about his uncle.

He failed, of course.

Mickey's ghost lurked in every corner.

Lisa arrived just after him, looking festive in a clingy red sweater and cream-colored slacks. Terry's excited laughter echoed through the rooms. Elena's eyes shone as she listened to the boy. And Marta was singing in Spanish, her pure, true contralto providing a cheerful background for the gathering. The delicious scents of roasting turkey and pumpkin pie spices mingled in the air. Even without tables full of guests, it was like every Thanksgiving Will had known, yet it was completely, fundamentally different.

Will did his best to ignore his memories. He kissed Elena. He told Lisa she was beautiful and earned another of her dazzling smiles. He teased Terry and helped Marta carry heaping platters from the kitchen to the dining room. He did just fine until the turkey was placed in front of him at the head of the table. Only then did he realize how difficult it was going to be to take Mickey's place. His heart pounded as he lifted the knife over the golden-brown meat.

Before he could make a slice, Terry said, "You forgot something, didn't you, Will?"

"I know you want one these great big drumsticks," Will returned, managing to smile at the boy's eagerness.

"I mean, the blessing."

Will's mouth went dry. Elena's smile froze. Marta and Lisa exchanged a troubled glance.

When Will couldn't seem to formulate a reply, Lisa said, "We're all too hungry to wait this year, Terry."

"But Uncle Mickey told me Thanksgiving wasn't about stuffing your face," Terry protested. "He said no one should eat without thanking God for freedom." The statement was a simplified but accurate summation of one of Mickey's favorite subjects.

"Then you say the blessing," Lisa suggested.

Terry shook his head. "Will should do it. He's cutting the meat. He should say the blessing."

In the silence that followed, Elena murmured, "I'll do it, Terry. It's the owner of the house who should bless the meal." Her dark eyes were deep tortured pools, but she laid her hands on the table and bowed her head.

Will saw that everyone else did the same. He couldn't. He stood unmoving while Elena repeated Mickey's special blessing.

Her voice shook, but the words were clear. "There are places in this world where a man can't feed his family. There are lands where there is no freedom to gather as we are doing here today. We are lucky to live here, lucky to have this meal before us. As we eat, we will thank you, dear Lord, for the richness of our lives, for the freedom we take for granted. To You, we give all praise." Elena crossed herself, then whispered, "Amen."

The word was echoed around the table by everyone but Will. He remained as he was, knife poised over the turkey, while his gaze locked with Lisa's. He knew she could read his every thought.

This hurt will pass, her glance said.

I don't believe you, his heart answered.

Finally, Terry lost all patience and demanded, "Cut it now, Will."

He did so. Clumsily. Without the finesse Mickey had always applied to the task. But he got through it. He got through the entire meal. He managed to laugh and talk. And he tried to ignore the specter of Mickey that hung like a pall over the table.

He felt Mickey's presence. Or his absence. Will couldn't decide which was the more accurate description.

Elena talked about the man so freely. Will didn't know how she could do it. As they lingered over their dessert, she told stories about past Thanksgivings. About the group of street people Mickey had brought in one year. About the time he and Will had gone to a wild turkey shoot and come home with a bird for Marta to pluck.

Didn't she understand what Mickey had done? Very soon she could lose her home, the last vestiges of her dignity. Yet she sat there, recalling her husband with a fond expression on her face.

Go away, Will raged at the ghost in the corner. *Go away and leave us with our misery.*

When Elena launched into still another tale, he stood, his chair scraping across the hardwood floor. Silence fell in the room as everyone turned to him. The rage he had held in such careful check around Elena bubbled over. "How can you do this? How can you talk about him like he's a saint or something?"

Lisa got up, took his arm. "Will, please—"

"I just don't get it. Elena, how can you talk about all the friends that filled this room on those other Thanksgivings? If any of those people were our friends, where are they now?"

Elena lifted her chin as she faced him. "They aren't here because I didn't invite them."

"Even if you had, they wouldn't have come." Will threw his napkin on the table. "He ruined that, too, Elena. He disgraced us, dishonored us. His name doesn't deserve to be spoken in this house."

Instead of waiting for a reply, he turned on his heel and stalked through the house, away from the lurking memories. Outside in the cold, he flung himself into an iron patio chair. He took deep, gulping breaths of the evening air.

Lisa joined him nearly an hour later. Her first impulse had been to follow him outside after his outburst. But she knew he needed some time alone. Elena had agreed.

The older woman had been surprisingly calm after Will's outburst and departure. "He's angry," she had said to no one in particular. "It will pass."

Terry had been more upset than anyone. He just didn't understand why Will was so mad. Lisa had tried to explain it to him yet again, but she feared she had made little progress. Finally she had sent him to watch a holiday movie with Elena. Lisa went to help Marta with the dishes.

Elena's housekeeper, another Cuban immigrant whom Elena had met through her church, had been like a member of the family for more than a decade. Besides her ready smile, Marta had a calm, no-nonsense attitude that Lisa had always admired. The two of them worked companionably, setting the kitchen right. When the last piece of Elena's best silver had been dried and put away, Marta pulled a bundle of letters from a nearby shelf and thrust it at Lisa. "Take these out and show them to Will."

"What are they?"

"Letters. Elena hasn't been taking many phone calls lately, but people have written."

Lisa took the rubber band off the bundle and sifted through the letters. There were more than twenty.

"Read a few," Marta suggested. "I know Elena won't mind. She shared them with me. One by one, every afternoon, I've been helping her with the replies."

Lisa had read. Now she stepped through the door from the kitchen and snapped on the patio lights. Will looked up in surprise as she dropped the letters into his lap.

"Not all of those friends you're so worried about have turned their backs on Elena. She had at least ten invitations to Thanksgiving dinner, Will."

He sifted through the letters, holding the envelopes toward the light to read the return addresses. Finally he bundled them together again and tossed them onto the low, white iron table between the chairs. "I'm glad to see Mickey didn't ruin everything. Now if all these good people would give Elena some cash, she might

make it through the next twenty years without him."
He looked up when she didn't reply. "What's the matter? Aren't you going to tell me my attitude sucks?"

"No, I'm not." Clutching her jacket around her against the cold, Lisa took a seat in the chair opposite his. "In fact, what you said in there was one of the few honest reactions you've had in the past couple of weeks."

"But I know I hurt Elena."

"I think she was glad that you unbent enough to say something you really felt."

"I've told you how I felt from the start. I hate him," Will said bluntly.

"You made that pretty clear. Even Terry got the message."

"I'm sorry about that."

She shrugged. "Terry isn't the one with the problem right now. You are."

"Well, my problems aren't the kind you can solve with an extra helping of ice cream or a pat on the back."

"You could try talking about them."

This conversation was exactly what Will had been hoping to avoid. Stubbornly he shook his head.

Lisa sighed and sat back in her chair. "Why is it that holidays are so tough for families? You know yourself that the department will have more domestic disturbance calls from now until New Year's than at any other time of the year."

"I think everyone just tries too damned hard to be happy." Maybe that's what he had done today, tried too hard.

"The first few years after my parents died, I thought the holidays should just be canceled."

"I'm not so sure that's a bad idea."

"Since I was an only child, I missed them worse then than at any other time of the year." She laughed slightly. "I remember being *so* angry that they weren't here with me."

"You were only nineteen or so when they died, weren't you?"

She nodded. "I was in college, had the world at my feet, as they say."

"I can see why."

She looked up and smiled at the admiration in Will's gaze. "I think I was an insufferable little Pollyanna, if you want to know the truth. I had an overabundance of confidence. My parents were older when I was born, you know, and I guess they were at peace with themselves or something. Anyway, they managed to make me into a pretty secure person. And then they died." She frowned, swamped by memories of that awful time. "Within ten months of each other, they were gone. I felt as if the foundation of my life had turned to quicksand."

Will knew that sensation all too well. "It must have been hard on you."

"I went a little nuts. And the guy I was dating at the time..." Her mouth thinned. "Well, let's just say he wasn't the most supportive person in the world. He was young, too, and he didn't know how to deal with my depression." She shivered and tugged her jacket tighter around her.

"That was the worst holiday season of my life. I spent Thanksgiving all alone, holed up in my parents' empty house. I was most angry with my mother. Dad had died suddenly, of a heart attack, and in my illogical, immature way, I thought that it was fate or something. But Mother hadn't been really well for a few years. I kept thinking that if she had just taken care of herself, if she had watched her diet or exercised more, then she wouldn't have left me alone, and I wouldn't have been forced to sit at a friend's house at Christmas, pretending to be part of someone else's family circle."

He understood the pretending. "It sounds pretty lonely."

"I think it wasn't until Terry was born that I began to forgive Mom for dying."

Distressed by the break in her voice, Will sat forward and put his hand on her knee. "You miss her, don't you?"

"Of course, I do," she said, steadying her voice. "I miss them both. The same as you miss Mickey."

With a muttered oath, Will stood.

"Don't bother trying to deny it. There's a hole inside of you big enough to swallow you if you let it."

He knew she was right. It was the void inside him that he kept trying to fill with anger. He couldn't let any of that anger escape or he would fall down into the black empty space in his heart.

"Okay," he said, turning from Lisa. "You've made your point."

"This isn't about making points."

"But you've made a few. You can be pleased about that."

"I'm just trying to be your friend." She pushed out of her chair. "We're all trying to be your friends. But you seem determined to keep us from it."

"Lisa—"

"It is truly easier to face alone?" she murmured, stepping toward him.

"No, it's easier not to face it at all."

"But that's impossible." She touched his arm, forced him to meet her gaze. "Remember how it was for me after I was shot, Will? I was so miserable, with all this fear and anger locked up inside me. I couldn't admit to any of those feelings, of course. If I admitted them, then everyone would point at me and say, 'Look, we always knew Talbot was just a wimp, just a woman who thought she was tough enough to be a cop.'"

"No one said that about you."

"But I thought they would." She laid her hand against his cold cheek. "You helped me through that. You made me admit my feelings. And when I faced them, they weren't so bad, after all."

His hand covered hers and drew it away. "This isn't the same, Lisa."

Her mouth tightened. "Why is it you're punishing all of us for what Mickey did?"

"Punishing *you*?"

"Me, Elena, Terry, Andy—all the people who care about you. Mickey's the one who hurt you, but we're the ones *you're* hurting now."

"Until this I.A. mess is cleared up, you and Andy are better off not associating with me."

"Isn't that a decision we should make?" Anger had put color in her face, snapping lights in her blue eyes. "I mean, really, Will Espinoza, who put you in charge of our lives?"

"I'm responsible—"

"No, you're not," she cut in. "You're not responsible for what he did. The only person you can control is yourself. And let me tell you, you're making some lousy choices these days."

"Now who's trying to control whom?"

"I don't want control," she denied hotly. "I just want you to realize that you don't have to go through this alone." Her laugh was tight with fury. "If you think back a few weeks, you might remember that you and I had something together. You were part of my life, of Terry's life. A big part." Her voice broke on the last word.

Will took her hand. God, he didn't want to hurt Lisa. "You're so important to me..."

She jerked away. "No, I'm not. If I were important, you wouldn't be pushing me away."

He stared at her in silent misery, then said, "I don't know what to say or do, Lisa."

"You could start by living again. I know it's only been three weeks since he died, since he betrayed you. But sometime soon you're going to have to go on with your life."

"I'm trying to."

"No, you're not. You're just sleepwalking. It's time to wake up and get back to your life."

"And how do I do that?" he demanded, his own anger surging forward again. "My whole life is based on his. I care about people because he taught me to. I'm a cop because he was. He is part of me, and his heart was as black as hell. How do I live with that?''

She backed away from him. ''Isn't it funny? I always thought you were your own person, not a reflection of him. I thought the importance of being yourself was the biggest thing Mickey ever taught you.''

He closed his eyes, wondering how she was able to target the core issue. ''You're right,'' he said, looking at her again. ''I always have been my own person. The only problem is that I'm not sure who that person is right now.''

''There are people who can help you find him.''

He turned away, thrusting his hands deep into his jeans pockets. He was suddenly aware of the cold. His deep, numbing anger had insulated him from the chilly evening air, just as it had sealed off all other feelings for the last few weeks. Every time the anger started to crack, he patched it up again. He didn't know if he would ever be able to let it go.

Behind him, Lisa repeated her earlier advice. ''You have to start living again, Will.''

''How do I do that?''

''You stop running away every time someone or something reminds you of what Mickey did.''

He felt her move closer, but he didn't turn. He could feel her waiting for him to reach out to her. And he couldn't. He still felt as if he could fight his inner demons all by himself.

''I guess I see how it is,'' Lisa said. Her voice was shaking, from anger or hurt Will didn't know. He couldn't turn around to see her expression. ''Last week, Elena told me you had always been stubborn and egotistical and hard to fathom. Well, she's absolutely right. Only I hadn't seen that side of you until now." She paused to catch her breath, but then went on. "There's just one thing I want you to know. The next move is up to you. I'm through trying to reach you. You know where I am. Call me if you ever decide to return from the dead."

Leaving Will on that patio was one of the most difficult things Lisa had ever done. Though they had parted in anger many other times in recent days, she knew this was different. She had issued him an ultimatum. It wasn't her usual style. When she cared about someone, truly cared, she usually had an abundance of patience. But she was exasperated with Will.

So she went inside, said her goodbyes to Elena and Marta and took Terry home. She went to work the next day. She took Terry roller-skating on Saturday. On Sunday, they decorated the house for Christmas.

She knew it was too early to put up a live tree, but Terry wanted it, and she didn't have the heart to say no. As he had grown up, Christmas had become a more difficult time for him. Perhaps it was because there seemed to be families everywhere you looked. At the mall. On television. There were children, mothers *and* fathers. Shopping together. Picking out trees. Terry seemed to miss having a father most during the holidays. The last two years, Will had made a real difference. Together, he and Terry had hung the wreath over the mantel and strung lights on the front porch. Together, they had picked out Terry's gift for Lisa.

Terry didn't understand why things were different this year. He wanted to ask Will over to help, but of course that was one area where she couldn't indulge him. She was sticking to her decision. Will would have to call her.

After decorating all day Sunday, Lisa and Terry perched on the edge of the living room sofa and surveyed the results of their Christmas handiwork. Their tree, a nine foot fir that had cost Lisa twice what she expected, shimmered with lights and tinsel in the corner. Wreaths were hung over the mantel and on the front door. The Christmas cards they had already received were taped to the railing of the stairs. The lights wound around the porch railing gleamed through the front windows.

Terry looked pleased with himself. "Old Will's gonna be impressed when he sees those lights I strung without him."

"Yeah," Lisa agreed as she let her tired muscles relax into the sofa cushions. There was no point in reminding Terry that Will might not even see the lights.

But Terry let her know Will's absence still bothered him. "I still think Will would have come over if I had called."

"He will call us when he can."

"Is he mad at me?"

"I've already told you a dozen times that he's not."

The boy seemed to mull that over for moment. His next words surprised Lisa. "I think I hate Uncle Mickey."

She sat forward enough to look into her son's face. "Why do you say that?"

"Because he's the reason why Will's staying away from us."

"Does that mean you have to hate Mickey, too? You used to like him an awful lot. Maybe you're just missing him, the same way Will is. You don't have to hate him because he's gone."

"But everything was better before he died."

She squeezed his shoulder. "It'll get better again. I promise." She also *hoped*, but she didn't let Terry know she had any doubts.

He nestled against her side, and for a moment she breathed in the familiar, little-boy scent of him. He was growing up so fast. In less than two months, he would be ten. He was bright and strong and healthy. Even without a father, he was doing just fine.

But the men in his life were on his mind tonight. He sighed deeply and confessed, "You know, Mom, sometimes I think I hate Dad, too."

She put her arm around his shoulders and hugged him, but made no reply. She thought it better to let him talk.

"Most of the guys at school have fathers. Even the ones whose parents are divorced get to see their dads. It makes me mad that mine doesn't want to see me."

Lisa realized that all her talk about Rich being too far away just didn't wash anymore. Their son was far too perceptive for that. He knew Rich could be with him if he wanted. Her throat was tight with unshed tears. She could only imagine how his father's rejection must hurt Terry. The only good thing about the situation was that he no longer thought she was lying about Rich.

"I guess I don't hate him, really," Terry continued. "I just want him to be here." He tipped his head back and looked up at Lisa. "You know what Jeremy thinks?"

Jeremy was Terry's best friend, a child whose imagination had always astounded Lisa. "What?"

"He thinks Dad might be a secret agent and that's the reason he can't come see me."

So, she thought, he wasn't really ready to accept that his father just didn't want him. "Do you think your father is a secret agent?"

Terry shrugged. "There are secret agents on television."

"Terry," she said, hugging him again. "Your dad is a computer engineer."

"Maybe being an engineer is just his cover."

She was amazed at how well he and Jeremy had thought out this fantasy. "His cover?"

"Yeah, on television secret agents always pretend to have another job so no one can figure out what they're really up to."

"I think you and Jeremy have been watching too many re-runs," Lisa said. "Your dad is just a plain old engineer."

Terry's eyes were big and blue and full of hurt. "Mom, can't I just pretend he's something else?"

She wanted to tell him no. Ignoring the truth could be dangerous. But that didn't seem to matter as she looked at him now. She ruffled his hair, drew him back on the sofa with her. "Okay," she whispered against his hair. "You can pretend for now."

For the first time in a long, long while, he sat in her arms until he fell asleep.

It was only after she had roused him and got him off to bed that Lisa was struck by the similarity of Terry's and Will's situations. Like her young son, all Will really wanted was for Mickey to be here, for everything to be magically right again. Because that couldn't be, he was angry.

But what was Will pretending? she thought, carrying the comparison further. The answers were simple. He was pretending not to need anyone. And just as she had allowed Terry to have his little fantasy, she was buying into Will's pretense, too. She was staying away, letting him tough it out alone.

That was agonizing. But she still couldn't give in and reach out to him again.

She did, however, hope Will would appear at her kitchen door or that he would call.

But during the next, long week, the only people who came through the door were herself and Terry. At the end of each day, she picked him up at the YMCA where he played after school, or she came home to him and his sitter. The only calls they received were from other friends. The hang-up caller struck again, but only once. Lisa hoped that caller was growing tired of his little game.

She was tired, bone-deep weary. Her caseload at work was growing steadily, but there were times when she felt overwhelmed by the details. She wasn't resting well. Her sleep was often disturbed by nightmares.

At work, too, she knew the rumors about herself and Will hadn't completely died down. The knowledge came from the way certain people watched her, and she couldn't deny that their scrutiny made her nervous. But she had also realized there were other people who didn't believe any of the rumors. She hoped Will had realized that, too.

She hadn't heard anything more from I.A. She wondered if they were making any progress in figuring out who might have been on the take with Mickey. Hopefully any investigation of herself, Will and Andy was over. None of her friends or colleagues had told her if I.A. had asked any questions about her past record.

The uncertainty of it all sapped her energy.

But missing Will was the worst of her problems.

Finally, at the end of the week, she went in to have a talk with the staff psychologist. Along with Will, Dr. Robyn Hastings had helped Lisa deal with the aftermath of being shot three years ago. She wasn't the kind of psychologist who listened to a person and then offered nothing more than, "And how do you feel about that?" In the past, she had offered more practical advice.

Today she let Lisa tell her everything that had been going on. Mickey's suicide. The I.A. probe. Will's withdrawal.

At the end, Dr. Hastings sat for a moment, her brown eyes studying Lisa. "You realize that with all you've told me, you've barely touched on your feelings. It's all been about Will, about how all of this has affected him."

Lisa shrugged. "I guess that's because the way it has affected him has definitely affected me."

"Do you love Will?"

The question caught Lisa off guard. "As I told you, we're involved—"

"But do you love him?"

Lisa couldn't give an answer. She cared deeply for Will, desired him as a lover, but she had never labeled her feelings as love. "I guess I can't give you an answer," she told Dr. Hastings after a few moments. "Why?"

"I just wanted a clear understanding of your relationship with him."

"Right now there is no relationship. And I really, really miss him."

"You're doing the right thing," the doctor said quietly. "I know it's hard to accept, but you can't solve Will's problems for him. You're a goal-directed person, Lisa, and you have a generous heart. Those are good qualities, but unfortunately there are times when they're also a liability for you and for the people you love. You like setting things right too much."

Lisa's smile was rueful. "I never thought of that as a fault."

"It isn't all the time. But in this case, with Will, there are some things he has to work out on his own. The person he trusted more than anyone in the world betrayed him. He is struggling to get a foothold on what happens next. Your pushing him to accept matters and get on with his life is a good plan, but he just can't do it yet."

"So my little ultimatum was pretty cruel, right?"

Dr. Hastings smiled as she shook her head. "On the contrary, some time away from you may be just what he needs to realize how important you are to him."

Lisa left her office feeling a little more hopeful. She was determined that if Will got in touch with her, she was going to be upbeat, cheerful. She was going to talk about Mickey only if Will wanted to. Instead of pushing him to deal with the issues, she was going sit back, let everything evolve naturally.

On Monday, she returned to work after what had felt like the longest, loneliest weekend ever. Will hadn't called. Lisa had finally broken down and called Elena, just to find out how he was. The older woman was very unhappy that Will and Lisa weren't seeing each other at all. But she said she understood the reasons why Lisa had backed away. After all, she was the person who had told Lisa not to coddle Will.

Lisa sat at her desk, remembering that conversation with Elena and surveying the stacks of paperwork before her with dismay. One of the department clerks came through with the mail and dumped another pile in Lisa's In basket.

"Gee, thanks," Lisa mumbled. Then she spied the square white envelope on the top of the stack. Her name was written in a slashing bold script. Will's handwriting. Heart jumping, she tore it open.

Inside was a plain white card. The note was simple.

You said I had to make the next move. So... how about dinner?

She was still staring at the note a few minutes later when the phone rang. It was Will. "Did you get it?" he asked without preamble.

"Yes."

He paused, and she pictured him running his hand along his jaw, perhaps thrusting his long fingers through his hair. "Well?"

"I'm waiting on the rest of the invitation."

He sighed. In relief, she thought. "Dinner at seven tonight."

"I'll be waiting."

Chapter Six

He should write a book, Will decided as he pulled his Camaro to a stop in Lisa's driveway. He would call it *Ten Days Without Her*. Critics would hail it as a dark, enigmatic tale of one man's loneliness. Woody Allen would most likely turn it into an introspective study of the average man's dependence on a woman. And when asked about his success, Will could tell interviewers, "I'm just glad it was only ten days."

"The longest ten days ever," he muttered, cutting off the engine.

He wasn't sure what he was going to say to Lisa. Nothing had been solved in the ten days since they had seen each other. Elena had put her house up for sale. A friend on the Narcotics Task Force had told Will that I.A. had come asking questions about his performance while on that team. And as an added bonus, the jerk of a lieutenant on his shift had mouthed off at him today.

Despite his troubles, however, all Will had known when he sent Lisa that note was that he would go insane if he didn't see her soon. He had planned to call her as soon as he went off duty, but in the end he had called her from a noisy booth beside the road. Just the sound of her voice had him smiling like some goofy, moon-eyed kid for the rest of the day.

"So go inside," he told his reflection in the rearview mirror. "You'll think of something to say." There was no reason to be so damn nervous.

Finally he took a deep breath and went to her front door. Not the back door, as had been his custom in the past. For some reason, the back door seemed too familiar.

Lisa opened the door before he could ring the bell. Dressed in something creamy that clung to each dip and curve of her body, she conjured every lascivious thought he had ever confessed in his altar boy days. At the same time, Lisa managed to remind him of the Christmas angel on top of Elena's tree. Her skin was the same flawless porcelain. Her hair the same spun silver-gold. She left him fumbling for words.

And she laughed at his discomfiture. "Are you coming in or do we have to stand out in the cold like the last time I saw you?"

He followed her inside and shut the door. "I guess I was expecting Terry to open the door and come running out."

"That's exactly why I sent him away. He's having dinner with his favorite sitter's family and after they eat, they'll come back here."

"The college student?"

"Yes, the pretty one with the five younger brothers."

Will grinned. "He may be only nine, but I do approve of the boy's taste in women."

Lisa put a hand on her hip, her expression mock serious. "So you've noticed Karen before, have you, Lt. Espinoza? You think she's a cute little trick?"

He took her other hand. "Don't you know I don't notice anyone else when you're around?"

She trailed one finger down his burgundy silk tie. Her lashes tilted down flirtatiously. "What about when I'm not around?"

"Then I'm thinking about you so much that other women go unnoticed."

Their lips drifted close, but Lisa swirled out of his arms. He brought her back with a firm but gentle touch. And he kissed her. Without preamble or explanation. He just claimed her mouth. She opened to him, her tongue against his in a teasing, absorbing dance. When the kiss ended, he just held her, his arms folding her body to his as tightly as possible. He breathed in the flowery, feminine scent of her. Pressed his face to the warmth of her neck. He had missed her so damn much.

She must have felt the intensity of his feelings, for she pulled away, her eyes dark with concern. "Will? What is it?"

He cleared his throat, trying to disguise the emotion he knew would roughen his voice. "It's been a hellish week," he managed at last. "Hellish."

"Forget it," she whispered. "Just forget this week."

Will made no promises. He just pulled her tight against him once more. He closed his eyes and pretended there had never been any angry words between them, never any distance.

"I think you need some champagne," Lisa suggested.

Nodding, he stepped back and for the first time took in his surroundings. The room, always comfortable, was especially welcoming tonight. Beneath the greenery-decked mantel, a friendly fire crackled, the flames reflecting in the crystal flutes and the waiting champagne bottle on the coffee table. Christmas tree scent hung in the air. Low, seductive music throbbed from the stereo system.

"Come on," Lisa suggested, taking his hand. "This bottle's been chilling for weeks."

He followed her to the couch. They sat close together, drinking champagne, talking mostly about inconsequential matters—the shape of the tree and the weather. They even touched on their jobs, but only briefly. Will was careful to skirt around the loud-mouth jerk and the I.A. He expected the conversation to become intense at any moment. He waited for Lisa to ask some of her typical probing questions. But none came.

Through it all, he wanted to take her hand, to say, "Let's start over. Let's pretend tonight is the beginning."

The words remained unspoken, but Lisa seemed to sense what he wanted. She was flirtatious and fun. She kept the mood light. After a glass of champagne, they drove downtown to her favorite restaurant, an establishment noted for its deceptively simple seafood and fresh fish entrées. They didn't accept reservations for dinner, and even though it was a weeknight, there was a wait to be seated.

Lisa and Will decided to kill the time in the revolving lounge that sat high above the city. The lights of Atlanta filled the night, twinkling and winking like a thousand eyes. Will had seen those lights a hundred times in his life. But they were different tonight. Friendlier, softer.

"Up here it looks so calm," Lisa murmured.

He nodded and surveyed the rest of the lounge's well-dressed occupants. "We're probably the only people here who know just how rotten those streets can be."

She sat forward, resting her chin on the heel of her hand. "Oh, I don't know, Will. There are probably lots of people here who have some deep, dirty secrets."

Deep, dirty secrets.

Her comment was offhand. Will was certain she hadn't meant to drag Mickey into their evening. But for one long startled instant he stared at her, and reality started to intrude on this perfect night. *No,* he thought, *I won't allow it.* He looked away, took a long drink of his seltzer water, and let the remark go unchallenged.

Lisa sighed. In relief, he imagined, and he felt pretty darn pleased with himself. What was it she had told him on Thanksgiving? *Stop running away every time someone reminds you of what Mickey did.*

Well, he wasn't running.

But he did feel claustrophobic. Again, he glanced around the room and at his watch. He looked at Lisa, who was staring out at the view, her mouth set in a tense line. "Come on," he said, standing. "Let's blow this place."

She blinked in surprise. "You promised me dinner, remember?"

"And you'll get it." He laid a few bills on the table to cover their almost untouched drinks and took her by the hand.

A half hour later they were digging into chili dogs, hamburgers and deliciously greasy onion rings at Atlanta's huge landmark diner, The Varsity. Neon rather than candle-lit, what the place lacked in subtlety, it made up in garish charm.

Lisa wiped ketchup from her fingers. "I can't believe I got all dressed up for this."

"I notice you've already downed half your burger."

"I was starving."

"Come on, admit it, you know you would rather be here than eating overpriced fish and steamed vegetables."

A smile crooked the very corners of her mouth. "Maybe you're right." She bit into an onion ring and closed her eyes in bliss. "Yes, you are *so* right. Much as I hate to admit it, Will, this is heaven."

Her choice of words sparked an idea. "Finish your dinner, gorgeous, and I'll really take you to heaven."

"Now that sounds promising."

He wiped a smudge of mustard off her chin and grinned at her coquettish tone. "You tempt me, Lieutenant, but we're going to the real heaven."

Their destination was actually Heaven's Open Arms. Housed in an abandoned school, the church-run recreation center was in one of the city's most economically disadvantaged neighborhoods. Lisa knew of the place, knew it had a reputation for good work. The center's organizers were intent on fostering a sense of community in the area's residents. They provided employment counseling and home improvement programs. They gave young people a place to hang out other than the streets. They were conducting an active assault on the problems of drugs and teenage pregnancies. Tonight, however, they were just making music.

Lisa could hear the choir from the street. Inside the center's shabby gymnasium, she found what had to be more than a hundred people, representing a full spectrum of ethnic backgrounds. All their voices were joined in a rousing rendition of "Joy To The World." In the center of the room was a piano. Though the instrument was well amplified, the pianist wasn't doing too well in keeping up with the choir's energetic vocalizing. Beside the piano, a short, wiry man stood conducting the makeshift choir.

Will and Lisa paused just inside the gymnasium doors. Leaning close to her ear, he said, "For years they've been meeting every Monday in December for a big community sing-along and food drive. Somehow, even on this side of town, they find a way to give. And on Christmas Eve, they open the doors and feed anyone who wants to come. Santa shows up. And they sing late into the night. Not just Christmas carols, either. I've been here when the music was rock and roll, gospel or jazz.''

When the last notes of the song faded, the choir took a break. Will led Lisa toward the center, where the leader was rifling through sheet music and muttering to himself. As they moved closer, Lisa could see the man was much older than she had imagined. But when he looked up and saw Will, his age-scarred face seem to lose years.

''My boy, my boy,'' he said as he pumped Will's head. His voice held the faintest trace of a lilting Irish brogue. ''What are you doing here?''

''I just took a chance you were still leading the Christmas community choir.'' Will turned to Lisa. ''This is my piano teacher. Mr. Pete O'Reilly.''

Lisa introduced herself. ''So you're the one who taught him to play so beautifully.''

''He had talent,'' O'Reilly proclaimed, nodding his grizzled head. ''He didn't like to practice, but he did have talent.''

Will gestured to the crowded room. ''I didn't make it by to see you last year. But it looks like the crowd is bigger than ever.''

The older man shrugged. ''I don't keep count. It's just nice to get out, to get into the Christmas spirit.'' He grinned and winked at Lisa. ''They could do this without me, but I keep showing up every year, and they don't have the heart to send me home again.''

''That isn't true and you know it.'' Will explained to Lisa, ''This man has worked hard for the center. He's raised plenty of money and also gives free music lessons. There are some talented musicians out there who owe their start to him.''

O'Reilly made a dismissive gesture. ''I've had to give up some of my work this year, Will. I've not been feeling the best. Had a touch of bronchial difficulties.''

Will surveyed him with a frown. ''Are you okay now?''

''As right as a soul can be at my advanced age. I just don't get out much.'' He turned as the woman pianist returned to her bench. ''Mary, dear, would you mind too terribly if this young man sat in for a while—''

''Oh, no,'' Will protested. ''I couldn't, really—''

''But it would please me so,'' O'Reilly said. ''Play a few and we'll sing along.''

The pianist had no objections. Lisa took a seat nearby. And for nearly an hour, Will coaxed incredible sounds from that old piano. He had thrown off his jacket. His tie was askew. The sleeves of his white shirt were rolled to the elbows. He was completely into the music. Now it was the choir who was challenged by the instrument's energy. But they responded well. While Pete O'Reilly beamed with happiness, the old gymnasium echoed with the sounds of Christmas.

Lisa didn't sing. She just sat, watching Will. She hadn't seen him look so content since Mickey's death. The music seemed to lift him. She felt at peace, too. They seemed to have started back toward the easy camaraderie they had once shared. The evening was typical of several of their previous dates. He had always done the unexpected—renting a limo to take them to a Braves game, surprising her with pearl earrings when it was no occasion at all. It was so like Will to start out at a pricey restaurant and end up in an inner-city community center. As long as he was here, there was nowhere else she would rather be.

She wanted the night to go on and on, but Terry was waiting at home with a sitter who needed to be home by eleven-thirty herself. Lisa had begun to fear she would have to interrupt and ask Will to leave when the songfest came to a close. And they were delayed even further by the dozens of singers who came forward to thank Will and ask him to return another time.

Pete O'Reilly didn't want him to go. "It does me good to see you, Will." His eyes were merry as he looked at Lisa. "Come back with your pretty friend next week."

"Maybe we can," Will said, shrugging into his jacket.

"And bring your Uncle Mickey, why don't you?" the older man continued.

Lisa sucked in her breath, darting a look at Will. His smile had faded, replaced by the stiff, cold mask she had come to know all too well.

O'Reilly hadn't realized anything was amiss. "Sometimes Mickey played Santa for us on Christmas Eve," he chattered on to Lisa. "He was perfect for the role, of course, but then if you know Mickey, then that's not a surprise. He's such a fine person, always ready to help a—"

"Mr. O'Reilly," Lisa cut in, unable to watch what his recollections were doing to Will for another moment. "I guess you haven't heard the news. Mickey is..." She swallowed. "Mickey passed away a few weeks ago."

"Oh, my goodness, no." The older man turned to Will. "My boy, I'm sorry. No one told me. And like I said before, I don't get out much. I don't read the papers, even. There's too much bad news. Oh dear, this is terrible news."

Lisa wasn't really too surprised that he hadn't heard about Mickey. The newspapers had policies about reporting suicides, and though talk was rife in the department, thus far there had been only a few news items about the scandal involving Mickey. She supposed in a city the size of Atlanta, one cop on the take was hardly a big deal. She knew if the I.A. probe eventually turned up others who had been involved, the media would probably get in on the act. She dreaded that for Will and Elena.

Right now, she watched as O'Reilly patted an ashen-faced Will on the shoulder. "It must have been sudden. What happened?"

"It was sudden," Will forced out, his eyes tortured. "Mickey—"

"—was in an accident," Lisa interrupted. She had no idea what Will had been about to say, but she'd be damned if she stood by and let him tell this man what had really happened. She couldn't bear to think how that would hurt.

"So sad," O'Reilly said, shaking his head again. "Mickey Vallejo was a prince. He'll be missed. Please, Will, give my regards to Elena. She's such a great lady."

"Thank you," Will said stiffly. He took Lisa's arm. "We really have to be going."

"Yes, but do come back."

Outside the gym, the cold night rang with the laughter of choir members going to their cars or walking to their homes. Snatches of Christmas carols drifted through the air, mixing with the sounds of traffic and a far-off siren.

Beside his car, Will paused. "There's nowhere," he muttered. "I can't go anywhere in this city where I'm not reminded of him."

Lisa tucked her arm through his, and leaned her chin against his shoulder. "I wish I could make it all go away."

Will's deeply drawn breath was a ragged sound. "But you can't. No one can."

"You forgot for a little while tonight. That's a step."

"I was lying to myself. There'll always be someone like O'Reilly in there, telling me Mickey was a great guy, reminding me of what a liar he was."

"But in so many ways he *was* a great guy."

Will's response was low and profane. "Please, Lisa, don't tell me that he meant well, that he stole to buy things for Elena, or that he must have been losing his mind."

"But all those things are true, I think."

"Pardon me if I refuse to canonize the bastard." Jerking his keys from his pocket, Will turned to the car.

Lisa forgot everything Dr. Hastings had told her about allowing Will to work things out in his own time. She wanted so desperately for him to learn to deal with this pain. She knew only then could the two of them go forward.

"It won't always be this way," she told him. "People will forget—"

"But I won't."

"I know it feels that way—"

He pulled open the car door and wheeled around to face her. "No, you don't know, Lisa. I don't think anyone has any idea how it feels to go through the days, my head so thick with memories of him that sometimes I can barely think. I keep hearing all he taught me. And just when I think I can handle it, just when I have a night like tonight, I realize all over again that he lied. Mickey Vallejo said he hated liars worse than thieves. One time he punished me, not because I broke a window, but because I lied about it. *La verdad es libre.* Truth is freedom. That's what he used to tell me, Lisa. But he's made me a prisoner of his lies."

She took hold of his jacket lapels, kept her voice low and earnest. "As long as you believe in what he taught, as long as you live that creed, then I can't believe that Mickey was a complete failure."

But Will was having none of that. "He's the villain in this piece, not a hero. Not my hero anymore."

"Are people always good or bad? Do you still believe that even after thirteen years as a cop?"

"I believe he was bad." Will's hands went to her shoulders. "He robbed me, Lisa. I keep trying to get it back, but he took the pleasure from my life."

"I promise you it will return. It came tonight, when you were playing the piano. While we were together." She moved closer. "I can help your pain go away."

Will's expression was beyond bitterness or sadness. Even the anger was missing from his voice. "No, you can't, Lisa. Even for one night, I can't look at you and not remember Mickey's gun in your face."

So there it lay, Lisa realized. Like a field of broken glass, all of Mickey's treachery continued to separate her and Will. Every time Will tried to cross it, he bled a little more.

Moments later, as they sped through the city toward home, she was assailed by despair. Instead of the teasing laughter that had filled the car on the ride to "Heaven," now there was only silence. No matter how she tried, there no going back to the intimacy she and Will had shared before this tragedy. Every so often there was a glimpse of daylight, but the dark always claimed them again. It made her wonder if what they had shared had been truly special at all. Maybe they had only friendship, made to seem something more by spectacular sex.

She didn't want to reduce their relationship to such terms, but she also kept coming back to what Dr. Hastings had asked her on Friday. Did she love Will?

Studying his bold profile in the light from passing cars, she asked herself why love had never been a word she used with regard to Will. She cared for him, respected him, desired him. But love? She didn't know.

Perhaps it was because she had loved him in a different way long before they had confronted their sexual feelings. He was her friend. She loved him as she loved Andy or Meg or her roommate from college. For any of those people, Lisa knew she would fight, would give of her time, her effort, herself. That didn't seem enough when she considered what she would do for Will. For him, she would give her life. And imagining a life without him . . . well, that was simply impossible.

So was that love? Lisa had little knowledge of the subject. Her first serious boyfriend had been the young man who had treated her so badly after her parents died. From the distance of eighteen years, she knew now that what she had felt for him was merely a replacement for the loss of her mother and father.

There had been no one else of any consequence until she'd met Rich. She had been struggling on the job then, trying to please some people who didn't think women had any business being cops. Rich had made her laugh, took her away from her professional problems. They had married too fast, had Terry too soon. It was only then that she had realized how selfish Rich was. He was jealous of Terry and even more upset when she refused to quit her law enforcement career in favor of being a full-time wife and mother. By that time, Lisa had achieved an equilibrium at work; she didn't want to leave what she had worked so hard to attain. She had been willing to compromise, but Rich had so little regard for her feelings or desires that she became stubborn. Locked in a battle of wills, their anger with one another had escalated. Rich's tantrums became so violent that one night he struck her. She had left him the next day.

Right now, she couldn't remember loving Rich. Every emotion she had ever had in regard to him paled in comparison to her depth of caring for Will.

But was that love? Did love hurt this much?

Lisa was still asking herself those questions when Will drew the car to a stop in front of her house. Every light in the place was burning.

"Something's wrong," Lisa told Will as she reached for the door handle.

Sure enough, Terry threw open the front door and ran down the sidewalk, barefoot and in his pajamas. Lisa caught him by the shoulders. "What's wrong? Where's Karen?"

But Terry didn't answer. "Dad called," was all he could say. "Can you believe it, Mom? My dad called me."

Over the top of her son's white-blond hair, she and Will exchanged a startled look.

Will stepped forward and put his hand on Terry's shoulder. "Come on, *amigo*, let's get inside before your toes freeze off." Terry went willingly, chattering with excitement about how his father had sounded, how he was coming for a visit soon.

Just inside the door, the young sitter stood, wringing her hands, her green eyes big and round. "I'm sorry he ran out like that, Lisa. He was too excited to sleep."

"Who called?" Will asked her as he shut the door.

Terry protested, "I told you it was my dad."

Lisa shushed him. "Go up and get into bed and don't come back down here."

"But Mom—"

"Now, Terry. Go. I'll come up in a minute and talk to you."

Startled by her tone, the boy fled the room.

Will turned back to Karen. "Now tell us what happened."

"I'm sure no one really called," Lisa said.

Karen's dark hair bounced as she shook her head. "Well, the phone did ring. Terry answered it in the kitchen about eight-thirty, and when I went in to check, he was talking to someone."

Lisa demanded, "Didn't you ask who it was?"

The sitter fell back a step. "Lisa, he sounded like it was someone he knew. I didn't know something was wrong. In about fifteen minutes he was still talking, so I went back to check on him. He was hanging up, and he said it was his father." Her eyes grew even wider. "I'm sorry if I did something wrong."

Lisa put a hand to her forehead. All she could think of was the hang-up calls she had been receiving. If tormenting a little boy by pretending to be his father was supposed to get to her, it was successful. She rounded on Karen again. "I just wish you had talked to this guy. It couldn't have been Terry's father."

"I'm sorry, I didn't—"

"It's okay, Karen," Will interrupted. "Lisa's just upset. I guess you know Terry hasn't seen his father since he was two."

The young woman looked so miserable, Lisa was consumed with guilt. "It's okay, Karen. You didn't do anything wrong. It's late and you need to go home. You're picking Terry up again tomorrow, right?"

Still apologizing, Karen got her coat and purse from a nearby chair and left through the kitchen. After she was gone, Lisa slipped out of her own tan woolen coat and walked toward the fireplace. The cheery blaze she and Will had left earlier in the evening had died to a few glowing embers. The room was chilly.

Behind her, Will said quietly, "It could have been Rich."

Lisa shook her head. "Rich would never call. He told me eight years ago that he didn't want to be part of Terry's life. and he's certainly never done anything since then to make me believe he could change." Loosening the barrette at her neck, she smoothed her hair out over the cowl neck of her sweater dress. "I'm sure Terry wants to believe it's his father—"

"But it is!"

The exclamation made Lisa turn. Terry stood midway down the stairs behind Will. His face red, he stood with hands clenched at his sides. She went toward him. "Honey—"

"It is my father. He said he was coming to see me."

Fear, cold as the night, licked through her veins. She thought of the ominous warning of her dreams, of the car that had been parked across the street in the middle of the night. She took her son's arm. "Terry, honey, what did this man say to you?"

He twisted away. "He isn't just some man. He said he was my father. He said he was sorry he hadn't been able to come and see me, but that he was going to make that up to me soon."

She caught him again, made him look at her. "Terry, even though this man told you that, he isn't your father. Somebody is playing a cruel joke on us."

"It isn't a joke. He's my father!"

"Terry," Will said. "Can you calm down enough to tell me exactly what he said?"

"I already did," the boy declared. "He said he was my father, and that he wasn't going away again, not ever. And I believe him, too. He won't ever go away."

Though it could have been her imagination, Lisa thought there was an accusation in the words her son threw at Will. Perhaps more than her, Terry had suffered from Will's absence from their lives in the last few weeks.

"You believe me, don't you, Mom?" he demanded now.

She chose her words carefully. "I believe someone called you, someone who said he was your father." Gently she brushed his hair from his forehead. "But no, honey, I don't believe it was really your dad."

Terry stared at her for a moment, his eyes narrowing. Then, without another word, he turned and ran up the stairs.

Lisa slid to a seat on the lower step and dropped her head into her hands. She felt rather than saw Will come to stand in front of her.

"Are you okay?" he asked.

Somehow she found the strength to look up at him. "Oh, yeah, I'm just peachy."

"Why don't you call Rich?"

The idea made her strength return. At her kitchen desk, she found the last number she had for him and dialed the phone with shaking hands. Even if it had been Rich, she was going to tell him a thing or two. He wasn't going to call up here and upset Terry for no good reason. The call went through, only to be answered by a recorded message saying the phone had been disconnected. Cursing, she slammed the receiver down.

"So he's moved," Will said after she explained. "You know where he works, don't you? You can call him tomorrow."

"I think I know the company. Rich has had five jobs since he left Atlanta."

"You mean to tell me you don't know where he works?"

The implied criticism in his voice snapped something inside Lisa. "I don't give a damn where he works. He made his choices. I'm the one who's had to explain things to that little boy up there. I haven't concerned myself with where Rich Talbot is hanging out."

"But what if something happened to you? How would anyone find Terry's father then?"

"Surely you don't think I'd want Rich to raise him. Rich doesn't even want him, for God's sake."

"You don't think he does."

"I *know* he doesn't," Lisa said, raising her voice. "You've got a lot of nerve second-guessing me like this."

Will raised his hands. "You're right, you're right. I'm sorry. I'm wondering who would be cruel enough to play this kind of horrible joke."

Closing her eyes, Lisa massaged her temples. "Oh, God, Will, you know there are always people ready to prey on small children." Her voice broke on the last word. She steadied it and went on, "I just hope they're not trying to get at me through him."

Silence greeted the last statement, and when Lisa opened her eyes, Will was staring at her, his face drained of color.

"Who?" he whispered. "Who would want to get to you?"

With chin lifted, she just looked at him.

Gradually, dismayed realization dawned in his expression. "Andy thought someone might try to hassle us."

"I still think he's wrong," Lisa replied. "But..." she went on to tell him about the car she had seen parked across the street and the hang-up calls. "Neither of those things prove anything, of course."

"But they might." Will's dismay gave way to anger as he slapped one fist against his other palm. "Damn! Why isn't I.A. doing something? The guys who were working inside with Mickey are walking around while we, the innocent ones, are being investigated and possibly harassed."

But Lisa still couldn't quite buy the idea that anyone would be harassing her. Even tonight's events didn't convince her. "What would they have to gain?" she asked, as she had been doing ever since Andy confided his fears. "I've told I.A. all I know." Dragging a chair out from under the kitchen table, she sat down in frustration. "We're jumping to conclusions. For all we know, Terry didn't talk to a man at all. Karen didn't hear who was on the phone. The caller could have been that crazy friend of his, Jeremy." She repeated Jeremy's outlandish theory about Rich really being a secret agent.

Feet apart, hands braced on his hips, Will demanded, "Do you really think Terry would resort to a fantasy like this, especially after you challenged his story?"

"He might. You know yourself that he's built some pretty tall fantasies about his father."

"But he has so many other people who care about him."

"Maybe he's not so sure about those people these days."

Lisa knew if she had thought about that remark, she might not have spoken. She certainly wouldn't have put such bitter resentment in her tone. But she was too tired to think, too weary to measure the impact of every word she said to Will. And it wasn't until the words had escaped that she realized how angry she was with him.

She had been trying so hard to be supportive of him, to understand what he was going through. But what about his responsibility to her? Damn it, he had made a commitment to her. Not a formal bond, maybe. Maybe what they had wasn't love. But the ties had been implied. And he was failing her. Failing her and Terry.

Will's face was even whiter than it had been before. "Lisa, I don't know—"

"Well, I *do* know," she cut in, giving her fury full rein. "I know there's a little boy up there who loves you. And he doesn't understand about Mickey dying and betraying you. He doesn't see why that has to change you the way it has." Her eyes filled with tears that she blinked furiously away. "All he knows is that you're letting him down. Good God, Will, every man in his life lets him down. That's why he might need to make up stories."

Now the tears wouldn't stop. She didn't want to cry. Tears were weak and pointless. But tonight she had finally reached emotional overload. The sobs shook through her in deep, wrenching bursts.

Crouching beside her chair, Will touched her shoulder, but she shook him off. "Please," she choked out. "Just leave. Leave us both alone."

"But I can't leave you like this."

"Why not?" she demanded. "You haven't been here for me lately. Why should a few tears change your mind about that now?"

"Lisa." He caught her chin, turned her face toward his. "I'm so damned sorry."

With tears still pouring down her cheeks, she studied him for a minute.

"I'm sorry," he repeated.

Her blue eyes, usually so warm, were cold. "No, you're not. You're lying. You're too selfish to be sorry."

The words hit him like a bullet. He sat in a stunned silence while Lisa turned away from him, her slender shoulders shaking with sobs. He knew he should put his arms around her, comfort her. But he didn't really believe that would make a difference. She had made it clear she wouldn't believe anything he had to say.

Dazed, he left the room and her house. His chest ached. His throat burned.

And he knew Lisa was absolutely right. He was selfish. He, the person who had always prided himself on being there for the people he cared about. He had let her and Terry down. He was letting everyone in his life down. Everyone. Andy, whom he kept putting off when he called. Other friends whose sympathy he didn't want to hear, people he was working with who had extended a hand in friendship. Even Aunt Elena, who deserved more than the morose silences and self-pity he had offered her.

Yes, he was failing everyone.

Just as Mickey had done.

The comparison brought a wave of nausea. Will had to clutch the side of his car as the sickness knotted his stomach. Mickey had prided himself on taking care of people, too. But in the final estimation, he had also let everyone down. Maybe Will had learned his selfishness from Mickey.

Just like Mickey.

The words rose like bile in his throat. God, he would rather die first.

With that last, angry thought, Will got into the car, turned the key and backed out onto the road with a screech of tires and a roar of the powerful motor.

Chapter Seven

A cold rain began to fall about five o'clock on Tuesday morning. Will, who hadn't slept, heard the first drops hit the redwood deck outside his living room. Sleet had mixed with the precipitation by the time he should have reported to work. He stayed home, phoning in at the last minute with an excuse. He had never missed a day of work. He kept thinking of the police motto, To Serve And Protect. For the first time in his career, he knew he was capable of neither.

He was so angry. That wasn't surprising. Fury had been his constant companion for more than a month. But this time the anger wasn't directed at Mickey, or Internal Affairs, or the people who seemed to regard him with suspicion. This time Will was angry with himself.

How could I have done this? he asked himself again and again. *How could I have hurt everyone so badly? Just as Mickey had done.*

Standing by the window with a cup of coffee in hand, he closed his eyes to the sleet and the rain, and he saw Terry's young, accusing face. He saw Lisa's cold blue stare. He felt their disappointment in him.

Throughout Will's life he had tried never to disappoint the people who mattered to him. Not that he had always succeeded. He wasn't perfect. He was far from that. But in the big ways, with the important people—his friends and his family and his fellow officers—he had managed to do the right things. Until now.

And now he had lost Lisa.

Yesterday he had realized that ten days without her was far too long. What was he going to do now?

She was better off without him, of course. He should be grateful that she had thrown him out of her life. Only two weeks ago he had determined to stay away from her until the I.A. investigation cleared her name. He should have stuck with that resolve. Away from Will, maybe Mickey's crimes wouldn't continue to taint her life. Without Will to remind her of what had happened, she could put the episode behind her and go forward.

And Will was better off without her, too, he told himself fiercely. She was a painful reminder to him, as well. Her life, mixed with Terry's needs, were too complex for him. She was far too direct, too pushy. She never knew when to let well enough alone. She was...all that he wanted. And now she didn't want him.

Groaning, Will sank down onto his sofa. *God, what a screwed up mess he had made of his life.* He couldn't blame anyone else for this mess, only himself.

He sat unmoving for the better part of an hour. The walls of his home were crowding in on him. Finally, when he could stand it no longer, he grabbed his coat and left.

At the times in Will's life when he had needed comfort the most, Elena and Mickey's house had always embraced him. He had found the same peace in Lisa's home. But that was closed to him now. Lisa was a part of his pain. Memories of Mickey were painful, too, and they rose to the forefront whenever he went to Elena's, but Will needed to return to a place and a person who had always made him feel good about himself. Somehow, he had to lose this sense of self-loathing.

But the For Sale sign in Elena's front yard mocked him with his failures. Elena shouldn't have to leave this place she loved, but Mickey had left her penniless save for a small pension and disability income. The expense of keeping up this house and paying Marta's salary were beyond her resources. Though Marta was as much friend as employee and had moved in, Elena insisted on paying her a small salary. Will could help, but his pay was typical of most cops'. There was a limit to what he could do. Selling and moving to a smaller house was the most sensible decision Elena could make.

Elena had been much more sane and reasonable about the situation she faced than Will. As he entered the house through the kitchen, he wondered where she got her strength. Except for the moment he had told her of Mickey's death, except for the night she had cried when he played for her, she had been strong and upbeat, even cheerful.

Today, he needed some of Elena's iron will, needed her wisdom, the understanding with which she had guided him in the past.

Marta was in the kitchen, but her ever-present smile was missing. In fact, she looked as though she had been crying.

Will surveyed her with concern.

"Don't worry," she said, summoning a smile. "It's just one of those days around here."

"Where's Elena?"

"In the living room." Marta sighed, her brown eyes very sad. As he started from the room, she touched his arm, warning, "She isn't herself today. Be kind."

He understood what Marta meant when he paused in the foyer outside the living room. Elena sat in her wheelchair before the front window, where a Christmas tree had been set up. No decorations festooned the branches, however. They were spread in boxes all over the room. Glittery bows. Gleaming balls. Garlands of tinsel. Will recognized the colors and shapes of his childhood. Though Elena had been able to do little decorating herself in recent years, she had always supervised. Will thought she took more joy in the season than any child he knew.

She wasn't joyful today, however. Her face was drawn, the effects of her illness in stark evidence. In her lap was the Christmas angel that reminded Will of Lisa. All cream and gold and shining, the ornament had topped Elena's tree for more than twenty years. Now she looked at it with abject sadness.

Will knew then that he wouldn't find the comfort he had come here seeking. But instead of taking from Elena, maybe he could help her. Maybe he could actually do something for someone who mattered to him. He swallowed the emotion that clogged his throat and stepped into the room. "Elena?"

She looked up, but without the smile he was accustomed to seeing. With her voice, however, she struggled to rouse herself. "Will, I didn't expect you."

"I'm playing hooky from work."

"Oh." Distracted, she looked back at the angel, her twisted fingers touching a gold-tipped wing with infinite care. "As you can see, Marta and I are decorating for Christmas."

He plucked a strand of garland from a nearby box. "Are you sure you want to decorate?"

She nodded, but he wasn't sure she had even heard him. She said, "Do you remember when I got this angel?"

"A long time ago, I know."

"You were twelve," she continued as if he hadn't spoken. "It was the first Christmas you lived with us. We decorated a tree in every room." Her sudden laughter bordered on giddiness. "Everyday, your uncle brought home another armload of new decorations. He must have spent a fortune." The light died in her eyes. "I wonder how he paid for them."

Will touched her cheek. "Don't, Elena."

"He bought me this angel," she murmured. "A beautiful angel for his beautiful wife, he said. I hadn't been beautiful in a long time, but when he said that, I believed him." Her eyes closed. "I believed in everything. And now it's gone."

Will realized at that moment that there was nothing he could do that would ease her pain. He sat with her for a long time, he allowed her to talk about Mickey, something he hadn't been able to do until now. But he didn't feel that he helped her.

And when he went home again, he felt worse than when he had arrived. He hated his helplessness. He felt as though he had lost everything. His aunt and uncle, his friends, his co-workers—they had been his family circle. And it was gone.

The pain and anger in his heart was like a bomb, ticking and ticking, winding closer and closer to detonation.

He forced himself to go to work the next morning. He did his job mechanically. The only time he felt any stirrings of life was when one of the patrolmen picked up an acquaintance of his for loitering.

Will was close by when a call came in that this guy had been hanging out at a local convenience store, acting in a suspicious manner and refusing to leave. The patrolman who responded to the call was a rookie working alone for the first time. He was a good sort, affectionately called The Kid by most of the shift. Will decided to swing by, just to see if he needed any assistance.

Once at the store, he recognized the loiterer as an ex-dealer. The man had been clean for years, and had become one of Will's best snitches when Will had been working on the special drug enforcement squad. But now he was down on his luck, between jobs, and he said he had been using the phone at the store to follow up on some leads. Will knew him and believed him. He recommended that the patrolmen send him on his way with only a warning.

The rookie, who had wanted to take the guy in, didn't like being second-guessed by his supervisor. Will finally had to get tough and pull rank on him. Evidently the rookie vented his frustration to the other lieutenant on the shift, the loudmouth jerk Will had been trying to avoid.

There was no avoiding him now. He caught Will in the parking lot after the shift ended at three. "Don't you think you were a little hard on The Kid today?"

Will, who was stowing his gear in the trunk of his car, just shook his head. He wasn't going to rise to this guy's baiting.

But the pugnacious lieutenant wasn't giving up. "What's the matter with you, anyway, Espinoza? Can't you even look a decent officer in the eye?"

Dull heat crawled up Will's neck. In his chest, the *tick, tick* of his heart accelerated. But he breathed deeply, and fixed the man with a steady regard. "Give it a rest, why don't you?"

"And what if I don't want to?"

Fury roared in Will's head, but he held on to his control and slammed his trunk.

The lieutenant laughed. "I told The Kid not to sweat it, you know. I told him that old druggie was probably one of your former employers."

Will steadfastly inserted the key into the front door lock.

"Is he, Espinoza? Is he one of the guys that used to pay off you and your uncle? I hear Mickey—"

Will never heard the rest of the sentence.

The bomb in his heart exploded.

And his fist connected with the jerk's ugly mug.

Lisa scowled when the phone on her desk rang late Wednesday afternoon. She should have left for home an hour ago, but there had been a rash of fires set in local churches. The public was justifiably outraged, and the leads, mostly farfetched and much too cold to follow, had been pouring in all day. She figured this was another one. But it was Andy.

"I hear he finally did it," he said in lieu of a greeting.

"Who did what?"

"So you don't know." Andy sighed. "Will took a piece out of the other lieutenant on his shift."

She lowered her head to her hand. "Damn."

"I knew it would happen sooner or later. He's been a fight waiting to happen for weeks. They should have made him take some time off."

"Is he okay?"

"He went to the hospital. It seems the other guy got in a few licks of his own. But it took three other officers to pull Will off of him."

She sucked in her breath. "How badly is Will hurt?"

"Some sore ribs is all I heard."

"What about the other guy?"

"Nothing serious. His jaw isn't broken, but I understand it'll be a while before he runs off at the mouth again."

Lisa shook her head. "He could charge Will with assault."

"There were a couple of people in the parking lot who are swearing Will was provoked. The captain down there wants it kept quiet."

"That's good," Lisa said. She understood how the law enforcement family worked. Most of the time, they pulled together to shield their own. The way the defense mechanism was kicking in proved that Will, despite Mickey's crimes, was still considered part of the family.

"But now Will's got time off whether he wants it or not," Andy continued. "I heard the captain went down to the hospital and told him not to come back until after the holidays."

"That long?" Even for an infraction this serious, it was a long suspension. Lisa knew it was for the best. But she could imagine how Will would resent it.

Andy said, "When you see him—"

"I won't."

There was a pause. "You *won't* see him?"

She picked up a pen and doodled on the legal pad in front of her. "I don't really think he wants to see me, either."

"What happened?"

"It's just..." Her shoulders slumped in weariness. She was too exhausted to get into all that had passed between herself and Will. "We just reached a parting of the ways," she finally explained.

"Which means he pushed you away one too many times, right?"

"I don't mean as much to Will as he does to me," she said, not bothering to hide her bitterness. "And I can't handle that anymore. Terry can't, either."

"I think you're wrong about his feelings. This is just a hard time—"

"And when will it be the right time?" she interrupted. "This has been a hard time for all of us. I'm sick of making excuses for Will. And if he's going to hurt me, I'd prefer he just stay away." Even as she said the words, she wondered if they were true.

"I don't think he'll stay away."

"Well, it's completely up to him. He knows where I live." Will had sought her out after her last ultimatum, but nothing had worked out as planned. So Lisa had little hope he would be back, especially considering all she had said to him that last night.

Andy cleared his throat. "Well, I just thought you should know about this..."

"Thanks. I'll call you." She started to replace the receiver, but then jerked it back. "Andy?"

He was still there. "Yeah?"

"If you see Will..." She took another deep breath. "If you see him, tell him I said..."

"What?" Andy prompted.

What message could Andy take him? That she loved him. She thought not. "Nothing," she finally murmured. "Don't tell him anything." And she hung up the phone.

It rang again almost immediately, and she snatched it up, hoping despite herself that it would be Will. But it was another lead on the church arson. As she had been doing for two days, Lisa forced herself to concentrate on the job at hand. She took down the useless information, pushed a button to send any further calls to the main switchboard and headed for home.

Only forty-eight hours ago at this time, she and Will had been sitting together, sipping champagne, trying to get their world on the right path again. Now he was alone somewhere, battered, and no doubt raging at the world.

But she couldn't think about that.

Maneuvering through the heavy afternoon traffic, Lisa switched channels on the radio and tried to change the direction of her thoughts. She had plenty she could think about. Terry was still angry that she didn't believe Rich had called. No one had called back, however. And Lisa's efforts to reach her ex-husband had proved futile.

The small computer company Rich had been working for in Oregon had folded some time ago. The landlord at the last address she had for him gave her a new address in another city. But he had left there months ago, too, with no forwarding address this time. His child support had arrived yesterday, before the tenth of the month, as usual. It was a money order, as was usual, too. And it was in a plain white envelope with no return address. Nothing strange about that. Rich had conducted their financial arrangement this way from the beginning. The postmark was from the same Oregon town she had last called. Lisa was certain she could find Rich if she tried a little harder. He couldn't have disappeared altogether.

But in truth, it would suit her fine if he did disappear, if he stopped sending her money. She should have stopped accepting it years ago. Each month, she used part of the cash to pay for Terry's after-school care and sitters. She banked the rest of it for his future education. She could take care of all of Terry's basic needs. She wasn't extravagant. Her house was paid for, purchased with money her parents had left her. She and Terry would do just fine if Rich never sent another dime.

Along with refusing the support, maybe she should have lied all these years, told him Rich was dead. That sort of finality would have been easier for Terry to understand. If only she could have brought herself to lie to him, Terry wouldn't be sitting by the phone right now, waiting for his father to call him back. Or pretending to wait. Lisa groaned. She didn't know what was worse—fearing Rich might have called, thinking that someone might be pretending to be Rich, or believing Terry had made up the entire episode.

At home, she found him in the living room, playing a video game. Sure enough, the cordless phone was on the floor beside him. Immersed in the game, he barely looked up when Lisa stooped to kiss the top of his head. "Have a good day, honey?"

He shrugged, and Lisa looked at Karen, who was gathering up schoolbooks and preparing to leave. The young woman shook her head when Lisa pretended to hold a phone to her ear. No one had called.

The night passed like hundreds of others. Lisa changed, made herself some dinner, coerced Terry into finishing his homework and did a few loads of laundry. It was nearly eleven before Terry was in bed and she could stagger to the couch.

Notes on the church arsons were piled in her brief-case, but she ignored them, opting instead to stare at the twinkling lights of her Christmas tree. Only then did she allow herself to think about Will again.

She loved him.

Lisa wasn't sure when that realization had been reached. She thought it had come sometime during the long night after he had left her in tears. Why her acceptance of love would come now, after the last horrible month, she had no idea. But here it was. She loved Will.

She loved him as he had been before Mickey's death—intense, eager for challenge, able to switch from serious to teasing at a moment's notice. But she also loved him as he was now—hurting, needful, made selfish by his personal struggle to accept Mickey's shortcomings. She loved all that Will was and could be, bad as well as good.

Yet she was glad she had sent him away.

Life was strange, she decided. She had thought herself content with the passion and camaraderie Will had offered her in the past. She had counted herself lucky that he trusted and desired her, that they could roll easily from one day to the next with each other. She thought she didn't need declarations of undying love. Now, however, when everything that was easy between them had disappeared, when being with her reminded him so painfully of Mickey's betrayal...now, she wanted his love. It was his love, or nothing at all.

She didn't know if Will was capable of love. Love began with trust. And right now, he didn't trust anyone. If he trusted her, he would be here now, the problems of the past month would have never occurred. If she had his trust, she could hope for his love. But she didn't. And she couldn't keep reaching out and being disappointed.

That's why it was better that she had sent him away. That was why, even though she ached to call him, it was best that she didn't. She was afraid that if she saw him, she would be tempted to settle for less than his love. Now that she was sure of her own feelings, it had to be all or nothing from him, too.

Headlights from a passing car swept across her front windows, rousing Lisa from her contemplation. It was late. She couldn't solve anything tonight. But as she crossed the room to draw the curtains, she realized the passing car lights hadn't really passed at all. Stepping to the side, she peered out the window. It was hard to see, but a car sat in her driveway with the engine running. A powerful engine...

All logic fled. She forgot that she wanted Will to stay away. She didn't think at all as she threw open the front door.

He limped up the walk. Limped, and looked at her with an expression she didn't believe she had ever seen before. It was yearning, she thought, deep, agonized yearning. She didn't try to guess what that expression meant. Clasping her hands together, she stood on the porch and waited until he reached the bottom step. Then they stood, just watching each other.

He looked terrible and yet wonderful at the same time. There was a bruise on his chin. Dark hollows under his eyes. His hair was shaggy, his old leather bomber jacket was unbuttoned against the cold, his blue jeans were tight and patched and worn. And he was looking at her as if he was afraid she would order him off her property.

Finally he broke the silence. "I know you told me to go away."

"I was angry."

"Are you still?"

She wanted to be. She wanted to use that anger as a shield against the love that was throbbing through her right now. She tried, fruitlessly, to think of all she had just decided. Will didn't trust her. He might never love her in the way she loved him. But none of those sane, logical conclusions mattered. Not when she looked into his dark beseeching eyes. All she wanted to do was love him, to take away some of his pain. She stepped to the edge of the porch. "I guess I can't stay angry with you."

He came up a step. "I tried to stay away from you. It would be better if I did, so I tried like hell."

She managed a soft laugh. "Be careful. You're going to make me mad again."

"Oh, God, Lisa..."

They met on the middle step, their arms wrapping around each other.

Will buried his face in her pale, fragrant hair. whispering her name again and again. The peace and comfort he had been seeking for days was finally his. "I've been so lost," he murmured. "So lost, Lisa—"

She captured his words with her lips. Softly, like a benediction, her kiss washed his agony away. He didn't want to need Lisa. For weeks now he had tried so damn hard not to need anyone. After he left the hospital this afternoon, he had gone home, had driven around the city, trying to think of a place where he could find solace for his battered heart and body. But there was nowhere. In this city he had called home for all his life, the only sanctuary he could think of was where he was now. In Lisa's arms.

He drew away, wanting to tell her what she meant to him, how sorry he was he had hurt her and Terry. But he couldn't think of any words that captured the fragile, silken melody that ran through him. He could no more explain how he felt than he might explain music to someone who had never heard it before. His feelings, like music, could only be shown.

So he kissed her again. He touched her face. Ran his fingers down the smooth skin of her neck. Like the notes of a familiar song, the pleasure of touching Lisa came flooding back. They harmonized for long, precious moments.

And the words came then, hastily whispered, sandwiched between greedy kisses.

"I've missed this."

"I thought staying away would make things simpler."

"It didn't."

"I've felt so empty."

"So have I."

"Forgive me?"

Her answer was a sigh, a sound that struck a chord deep inside Will. Ignoring his aching ribs, forgetting all the despair of the last month, Will reached for the sensual but teasing rhythm he and Lisa had had long before Mickey's duplicity had plunged them into chaos.

His muscles tightened, hardened, as his hands slipped down her body. Through the age-softened material of her sweatshirt, her breasts fit his palms so well. Rounded. Sweetly peaking.

Her breath caught on a gasp. "The neighbors—"

"—Are in bed." His mouth opened against her neck.

"No, they're—"

His tongue, moving lightly into the hollow at the base of her neck, ended that protest. Against his gently rotating thumbs, her nipples jutted and pebbled, and she groaned.

Will chuckled. "So much for the neighbors."

Lisa pulled away, laughing as she stepped up on the porch. "We're going to be arrested for public lewdness."

"Then let's make sure it's worth it."

She backed away. "Will—"

But she was trapped against the wall beside the front door. She protested again, feebly, but his kiss turned the words to a purr of contentment. He slipped his hand under her shirt.

"How do you do this?" she murmured against his mouth.

His hand gently kneaded her breast. "This?"

"No—"

"—This?" His mouth closed over hers again.

She pushed him away, backed toward the door. "I mean, how do you change gears so fast? One minute you're dead serious, the next you're seducing me on my front porch."

Sobering, he framed her face with his hands. The Christmas lights Terry had wound around the porch railing washed her face in rainbow hues. She looked so beautiful, as beautiful as ever. Yet fragile, too.

Did he imagine it, or were the planes of her face more pronounced than before? Had the violet shadows beneath her eyes always been so dark? He got hold of his guilt before it could grow. If he allowed himself, the regrets could begin, the thoughts and the feelings that had kept him away from her could intrude. He could fall out of tune with the happiness of being here with her. And he wasn't going to play it that way. Not tonight.

He summoned his smile, strove for just the right carefree note. "I want to laugh tonight, Lisa. I want tonight to be the way it used to be."

In answer, she took his hand and pulled him inside.

Quietly, so as not to wake Terry, they moved through the house. To Lisa's room.

It was as Will remembered. Filled with the best of memories. Fragrant as a springtime meadow. The door shut behind them, blocking out the world. The silk-shaded lamp beside her bed cast shadows on the deep blue walls as Lisa drew off his jacket, unbuttoned his shirt.

With gentle lips, she kissed the purpling bruise on his side. With infinite care, she undid his belt, slipped the zipper of his jeans downward. His erection sprang heavy and proud against her touch. His hand covered hers, folding her fingers around him. Excitement curled through his gut, forcing an impatient groan from deep in his throat.

But Lisa was setting the pace. With slow, tantalizing movements, she undressed him completely and eased him down onto the bed. Crisp and white, the sheets beckoned, welcomed his aching muscles.

But it was Lisa who was balm to the bruises deep in his soul. Naked, she slipped into the bed beside him, a cream-and-golden angel. But there was sin in her kiss. A siren's wicked promise in her quiet laughter. He answered the call with hands that cupped her breasts. With lips that teased against hers. With fingers that strayed to the dewy waiting cleft between her thighs.

She opened to his touch, became music in his arms. A sexy, steady drumbeat of touch and sigh, taste and whisper. The tempo was easy to follow, yet constantly changing. He moved against her. She moved against him. Fast and then slow. Then a repetition of the movement. Then slow and slower still. The tension inside Will stretched, held like an aria's final, soaring note.

When he was afraid his control would snap, Lisa slipped over him, took him deep into her body. Propelled by a crescendo of need, he stroked upward. Once, twice. Then there was release. Together they cried out their completion. The drumbeat slowed. Faded.

Breathless, her body covered with a fine sheen of perspiration, Lisa slid to Will's side. They lay together, their breathing gradually changing from ragged to normal. She turned on her side, laid a hand against his chest, looked deep into his eyes.

She had to swallow her instinctive words of love. What they had shared wasn't about love. Will had been seeking comfort in her embrace, a place to forget the troubles that plagued his spirit. Comfort wasn't love.

Comfort wasn't what she wanted, what she had promised herself she would demand from him. All or nothing, she had decided. How quickly she had forgotten.

Perhaps Will sensed the conflict brewing inside her. His voice was husky. "Is everything okay?"

No, she wanted to answer. *We haven't solved anything by making love. All we've done is push the world and all our problems to the side for a few precious moments.*

"Lisa?" he prompted as he turned to face her. The effort must have irritated his bruised ribs, for he groaned.

"Does it hurt?"

He shook his head. "Nothing can really hurt when I'm with you like this."

The words contradicted what he had told her Monday night. He had said then that just looking at her made him remember Mickey's gun in her face. Nothing had changed that. And someday that tragedy would rise between them again.

She lifted her hand to his mouth, traced the outline of his lips with her finger. Though she knew the answer, she was compelled to ask, "What made you come here tonight?"

Eyes narrowing, he focused at a point somewhere over her shoulder. "I felt so damn lost, like everything was gone—my family, my career." His voice roughened. "You."

"You never lost me. I told you to go, but I wasn't lost. I was just waiting."

He took her hand, pressed a kiss into the palm. "I know. I'm sorry. I've been trying to screw everything up."

The utter desolation in his voice twisted her heart. Did it really matter why he had come to her? She loved him. She wanted to heal his deep festering wounds. She had been trying to bind those hurts since Mickey had inflicted them. But she couldn't. Will had to heal himself, in his own time, in his own way. All that she could possibly hope to do was stand by his side.

For now, it had to be enough that he had come to her. She could worry about love, she could demand to know his true feelings. Chances were, however, that he didn't know how he felt. He was still a jumbled mess inside. What she had to hold on to was that he had finally reached out for her. Tonight, he had taken comfort in sex. She was smart enough to know sex was a tenuous bond, at best. But perhaps, by re-establishing the intimacy they had once shared, they had rebuilt one corner of the foundation Mickey had knocked out from under their relationship. Day by day, if she was patient, perhaps they would build the love she craved.

Until then, Will was here. That was a start. He was warm. Eager for her kisses. She might be only a refuge where he could hide from his pain. But that was more than she had been yesterday.

So she kissed him. And touched him. Together, they scaled the heights again. While Will moved inside her, she kept repeating to herself, *It's enough. It's enough for now.*

And in the quiet aftermath of passion, she curled her body around his and slept.

She woke sometime later. The bed was warm, but Will wasn't beside her. She peered at the bedside clock. Only four-thirty. She didn't have to get up and get ready for work for at least another hour. Sitting up, blinking, she glanced toward the bathroom, where a light gleamed around the half-open door. She waited, but Will didn't come out.

Thinking he might need something for the pain of his bruised ribs, she slipped silently from the bed and padded across the carpet. A short distance from the door, however, she stopped. Without speaking, she looked at Will.

Naked, he sat on the edge of her tub. Elbows on his knees, his hands covering his mouth, he stared down at the floor. His expression was bleak and forlorn. He looked like a man without hope.

She started to say something. It took all her strength to resist, to back away, to go back to bed. There was nothing that hadn't already been said a dozen times. If she waited, Will would trust her enough to share his pain.

She hoped.

Chapter Eight

Thursday evening, Will threaded his way through the group of boys who streamed from the YMCA gymnasium. The nine- and ten-year-olds were all sizes, colors and shapes, but not one of them was the boy he sought.

"Any of you guys know where Terry Talbot is?" he asked, stopping a trio who were fighting over possession of a basketball. They pointed back toward the gym, barely taking time out from their wrestling match. Grinning, Will pushed through the double set of heavy steel doors. Boys never change.

Inside, Terry was alone at one end of the basketball court, practicing free throws. A small group of older boys were practicing lay-ups at the other end. A man who looked like a coach approached Will.

"I came for Terry," he explained.

The coach nodded. "Terry's mother called, said you'd be coming for him this afternoon. I hate to do this, but I need to see some ID. We don't let the kids go home with someone we've never seen before without checking it out."

"No problem." Will flipped out his police ID.

The man perused the photo card and badge carefully before handing it back. "Thanks. Terry's mother asked us to be really careful regarding any strangers who might ask for him. You probably know there's been someone calling Terry."

"Yeah. You seen anyone hanging around?"

"Sure haven't."

"Keep an eye out, okay?" Will shook the man's hand, then crossed the court toward Terry. "Hey," he called. "You gonna practice all night, or do you want to have some pizza with me and your mom?"

Terry barely glanced his way. He shot a basket, retrieved the ball, shot again. The second time, however, Will scooped up the ball.

Hands on hips, Terry glared at him. "I thought Mom was picking me up at six-thirty." He pointed at a large clock on the opposite wall. "It's just six."

"I'm off from work for a while, and your mom asked me to pick you up early. Aren't you hungry? We're going to pick up a pepperoni with extra cheese on the way home."

Stubbornly, Terry stood his ground. "The coach says I gotta do better at free throws. I'm still practicing."

"But most of the other guys are gone."

"I want to practice some more."

Will tucked the ball under his arm and pretended amazement. "You want to practice more than you want pizza? I think I may faint."

Terry didn't crack a smile. He blew out a frustrated breath and started toward the bleachers. "All right. I'll go."

So nothing had changed since this morning, Will thought. When Terry had come downstairs for breakfast and found Will making eggs and toast, he hadn't greeted him with the enthusiasm of old. He was polite but wary. Now, even the politeness was gone.

"Hey," Will called after him. "Come back here."

The boy stopped, shook his head, then turned around with a long-suffering expression on his face.

Will dribbled the ball a couple of times. "I think we ought to talk." When Terry didn't reply or move forward, Will went to him. "I guess you're kind of upset with me, aren't you?"

Shrugging, Terry kept his eyes studiously on the floor.

Will crouched in front of him. "I know I haven't been around very much. I'm sorry about that."

Terry shrugged again and started to turn.

But Will very gently took hold of his arm. "I'm really sorry, Terry. I wish I hadn't let you down."

"At Thanksgiving, before you got mad at Aunt Elena, you told me we'd shoot some baskets together," Terry accused, finally meeting his eyes. "But then you hardly came around. Mom wouldn't let me call you."

"I know. I had..." Will paused, looked down the court. "I had a lot of stuff on my mind, you know. I had to be alone."

"Mom tried to help me a couple of times, but she's not very good at basketball."

"I bet you don't need much help. I mean, you made first string and all."

Terry's blue eyes were troubled. "But I won't stay on it if I don't get better. I'm shorter than the other guys."

"Size doesn't matter as much as speed. And you're pretty fast." Will stood, wincing only a little as his sore muscles protested. "Come on," he invited. "Let's shoot some baskets now."

"I thought we had to go."

"Your mom will wait."

Will knew he would pay for his exertions in muscles that would be even sorer tomorrow. But it was worth any price to try to make amends to Terry for his neglect over the past month. They shot baskets for another half hour, and though the boy seemed to appreciate the basketball pointers, he was very quiet on the way home. Will's inquiries about Terry's friend Jeremy, his schoolwork and his Christmas wish list were all met with monosyllabic answers.

Once he was home, the boy bounded into the kitchen, demanding of his mother, "Did he call?"

Lisa shook her head. Shoulders slumping in disappointment, Terry left the room and went upstairs.

"This is beginning to worry me," Lisa told Will. "Did he say anything about his father when you picked him up?"

Will set the pizza carton down on the table. "He didn't have much to say to me about anything."

"But you're awfully late. I thought maybe you went somewhere fun together."

Will explained what had happened. "He's pretty angry with me."

"Well, you have to prove yourself to kids."

"I'm going to spend lots of time with him," Will vowed. "God knows I have time on my hands these days."

Lisa slipped her arms around his waist. "We really didn't talk about the suspension last night."

Will grinned at her. "I don't remember much talk at all."

She pressed a kiss to his chin. "You're right."

"Maybe that's for the best."

"What do you mean?"

He shrugged. "It's just that last night seemed like old times. Let's not muddy things up with a lot of talk about things we can't change."

She turned from him, opening a cabinet door to take down a stack of plates.

"Lisa?" he prompted when she offered no comment. "I just want things to be the way they were between us. Isn't that what you want?"

With her back still toward him, Lisa closed her eyes. She knew, even if Will didn't, that things between them weren't the same. For he wasn't the same man he had been a month ago. The man she had chanced upon early this morning, sitting alone and dejected, wasn't the Will who had once been her carefree lover. And she was different, too. She had different expectations for their relationship, different needs. They would never be the way they had been before.

He came up behind her, putting his hands on her shoulders. "Is there something wrong?"

Mutely she shook her head and resisted the urge to tell him they couldn't hide from the past. She had decided last night to follow the advice Dr. Hastings had given her last week. Will must work through his own private demons. If Lisa wanted any kind of relationship with him, she couldn't push him for the emotional intimacy she craved.

"Lisa?" Will repeated.

She turned and smiled at him. "You're right. Let's not muddy things up with a lot of talk."

He kissed her. "I'm glad you see it the way I do."

"Good, then take these." She thrust the plates toward him.

"What are these for?"

"The pizza."

"You don't need plates for pizza."

"Yes, you do."

From the doorway into the hall, Terry called, "You guys have this same argument every time we have pizza."

Lisa looked at her son. He was actually smiling, something she hadn't expected after the way he had left them a few minutes ago. "What do you think?" she asked him. "Plates are necessary for all food, aren't they?"

"What's wrong with paper towels?"

With a triumphant smile, Will put the plates back in the cabinet. "Terry, my man, I have taught you well."

"You're a couple of barbarians," Lisa told them as Terry tore a long strip of towels off and carried them to the table.

Will caught Lisa in his arms and kissed her soundly. "You know you love barbarians," he growled. "Every woman does."

"Gag," Terry pronounced with the sensitivity only a nine-year-old boy could display.

The kitchen rang with laughter during the meal. It *was* like old times. And because it meant a lot to her to see Will and her son having fun together again, Lisa tried to push all her worries aside.

For more than a week, they slipped back into their old roles.

Lisa was busy at work. They had no breaks in the church arson case and two more locations had been hit in the past few days. She thought there was something they were all missing, something she should pick up on, but thus far, she was coming up empty-handed.

Her spare time was limited, but Will claimed it all. They Christmas shopped, visited with Elena, went back to Pete O'Reilly's community center for another Christmas sing-along. Will had his bad times, his silences, times when he didn't talk to her about what he was feeling. He tried to hide any negative emotions. There were moments, when, faced with his false gaiety, she wanted to shake him, tell him he wasn't fooling her. For someone like herself, who believed people should confront their fears, it was difficult not to push him. But she resisted.

She felt the strain even in her sleep. Her dreams were vivid and frightening. Sometimes she dreamed of

Mickey, but then he would change to the man who had shot her three years ago. But that wasn't the worst dream. In the worst, she and Will drove in a car on the edge of a cliff. Another car chased them, blocking off every attempt at escape. The cliff was crumbling under their wheels. They had started over the side when Lisa jerked awake. She lay, holding her breath, listening to the deep, even cadence of Will's breathing as he slept.

After each dream, she lay awake, afraid to drift back into that world where she couldn't control her thoughts or her fears. The lack of sleep was taking its toll.

Will commented on how tired she was, but she didn't tell him about her nighttime terrors. She prayed she wouldn't call out or wake him and be faced with explanations. What good would it do if he knew she wasn't completely over what Mickey had tried to do to her? Telling Will would "muddy things up," as he had put it.

For the most part she tried to keep things light and easy. Will seemed content with that. He was spending lots of time with Terry, picking him up from school, trying to re-establish old ties. Terry responded, but Lisa believed her son had lost some of his trust in Will. A few times, when she watched the two of them together, she was surprised to see a very adult look of skepticism on Terry's face. He was much more tentative with Will now. Much less open.

Will saw the difference. Late one night, he and Lisa sat before the fire at her house, talking about the way Terry had changed. "I feel like I've lost something with him," he said. "Something really important."

Lisa was afraid he was right, but she also hoped the damage wasn't irreversible. "Give him time," she urged. "He's the kind of kid who has to work things out on his own, you know."

"I'm trying to do that. But it's tough to realize that I'm not his hero anymore."

"But you are."

"No, I'm not," Will insisted. "I know Terry doesn't give his trust too easily. I abused that trust, and he's reluctant to give it again. I should understand. I was like that as a boy, too."

She squeezed his arm. "And look how you turned out."

He sighed. "Yeah, look at me—"

"Cut that out," she said, punching him playfully on the shoulder. "I sort of like you."

He grinned, leaned over and kissed her. "Only sort of?"

"Maybe a whole lot."

They smiled into each other's eyes for a moment, then Will sobered again. "Damn, Lisa, what can I do about Terry? It's bothering me that I can't make it right."

"I believe it will work out," she insisted. "You have to remember, Will, he's had a lot to absorb recently. You weren't here. I've been pretty upset. And . . ." She took a deep breath and mentioned the taboo subject. "Mickey's death has been hard on him. No one close to him ever died before, and he cared about Mickey."

"Yeah." Pushing impatiently to his feet, Will grabbed the poker and pushed furiously at the burning logs, sending a shower of sparks up the chimney.

After a few minutes had passed, he said, "Maybe I'll take Terry over to Elena's tomorrow. She needs some cheering up."

"She sounded okay when I talked to her yesterday. Has something happened?"

"No. She tries to be cheerful all the time, but sometimes I catch her in a down mood she can't disguise."

That sounded like someone else Lisa knew, but she drew no comparisons.

"Anyway," Will continued, "I think it will be good for Terry to spend some time with her. Maybe he has some questions about Mickey that she can help him with. I remember when I was a boy, she had a way of putting things into perspective."

"Perhaps she can," Lisa agreed, sighing. "I just wish he'd stop this nonsense about Rich."

Will poked at the fast-burning logs again. "While I've got lots of time, why don't I get on the phone and see if I can find Rich."

"No," Lisa said firmly.

"But what if he was the one who called?"

"And if he wasn't, I'll just have to be reminded that he doesn't want anything to do with our son."

Will glanced at her. "Remember, Lisa, this is about Terry and his father. Not about you and Rich."

"I know," she murmured, impatiently thrusting a hand through her hair. "It's just that I don't want to invent more problems. I mean, what if Rich did call? What if he wants to see Terry?"

"I guess you'd have to let him."

Just the thought was painful. "I don't know if I could do that." She refused to consider the possibility.

"I don't have to worry about this. Rich didn't call. If he had, why wouldn't he call back? I think that for some reason, Terry made the whole thing up."

"But he gets so furious every time you or I suggest that. He walks around with the phone in his hand half the time."

"I know, I know." Lisa sat forward, staring into the fire, as if the flames would magically give her the answers she needed for her son. "Do you think he needs help, Will?"

He turned to look at her. "Professional help?"

"A child psychologist or maybe the counselor at school."

"I don't know." Will considered the suggestion for a moment, feeling the familiar stirrings of guilt. If Terry needed help, it was partially his fault. He glanced at Lisa, whose face mirrored his own inner turmoil. She was really worried.

Damn, but he wished he could go back a month. Go back years. He wished he could pinpoint the exact moment Mickey had begun his slide into corruption. If Will could go back in time, he would find that moment, he would stop Mickey, and that would halt this entire chain of events. Mickey was the root of all their discord. Damn the man, anyway...

With some effort, he took hold of his runaway thoughts. He forced his anger to subside, fought his guilt, just as he had been doing for the past week. There were times when he felt like a powder keg, ready to blow, but he was conquering the impulse. He felt sure if he kept a lid on his anger, if he controlled his negative emotions, he and Lisa could get through this.

And when everyone had forgotten that Mickey Vallejo had existed, when the I.A. found his accomplices, when all the rumors and speculation had died away for good, then there would be a chance for them.

But a chance for what? As he crossed from the fire and sat down beside Lisa again, Will faced a question that had been eating at him for days. What did he really want from this relationship? He didn't know, couldn't allow himself to think that far ahead.

He did know that when he had sought Lisa out last week, he had been lower than at any point of his life. She had pulled him from the abyss. She and Terry had filled the emptiness inside him with something other than anger. The easy, everyday rhythms of their family life provided a calm counterpoint to the anguish that still gripped him from time to time.

The only thing he could compare it to was when he went to live with Mickey and Elena after his mother died. After the quiet, shuttered stillness of his mother's home, Elena's house had seemed so bright, so open, so filled with laughter.

Lisa's home was like that. Even though Terry wasn't back to his old self, simply being with him and Lisa was bringing Will back to life. He thought he understood how miners must feel when they emerged from underground. Sometimes he was startled by the sheer brightness of the world around him. He became depressed sometimes . . . hell, he still had his moments of despair. But now he thought there was an end to the darkness.

Lisa was the source of his light. She and Terry were important to him, more important than he had realized before Mickey's death.

Now he put his arm around Lisa's shoulders, drew her back against him, pressed his cheek to her smooth, pale hair. "Don't worry," he said. "Terry's going to be fine. If he needs help, we'll get it for him."

She lifted her face for his kiss. He meant the caress to give only comfort. But her response stormed through him, made him hard and aching. Soon they were locked in her room, his hands were on her body, he was in her. When they were together like this, caught in the sweet oblivion of passion, nothing seemed to matter, nothing could intrude on their world. When making love to Lisa, Will didn't have to struggle to block out his anger. Guilt and despair didn't exist when she was in his arms. Perhaps that was why his appetite for her was insatiable.

She welcomed him with a hunger that matched his own. At times, Lisa felt she was caught in a vortex of desire. She and Will had steamed up some windows before, but their earlier sensual exploits were nothing compared to now.

Always satisfying, but never predictable, their lovemaking was anything but tame. Often, it was hard and fast, edged with desperation. Will would look at her, and she would know he wanted her—*then*. Just the look made her moist and eager.

If they were alone, or Terry was in bed, Will tempted her into wild moments. On the bathroom counter, when they were supposed to be getting ready for Andy and Meg's Christmas party. Against the wall in the garage, where Lisa had gone in search of a stepladder. The sex at these times was elemental and explosive, devouring in its intensity.

But it wasn't always quick and raw. Sometimes they made love slowly, savoring each gliding touch, lingering over each taste, building easily toward completion. In the early morning, when they were both half-asleep. On Saturday afternoon, while Terry was with friends. These gentler moments were no less consuming, no less memorable.

When she was away from him, Lisa would think of the way Will had touched her, the dizzying, erotic words he had whispered, and her cheeks would turn red, her body would become flushed. She would ache from the excitement of just remembering. Then she would realize she was at work or in the line at the grocery store, and she would look around, hoping no one could read her mind.

These moments with Will, tender or rough, were memories she tucked away carefully. Like delicate crystal, stored in cushioned boxes, she knew she would someday want to take these moments out, hold them up to the light, rejoice in their clear, perfect beauty.

She didn't want to think this interlude of happiness would have an end.

On the Sunday evening before Christmas, they got Terry an overnight sitter and spent a long, romantic evening at Will's place. Actually, they had intended to go out to dinner, but when they stopped at Will's apartment for him to change, they became sidetracked. Pleasantly so.

Dinner was very late, after Will roused himself enough to pull on a sweater and jeans and go get sandwiches and fruit from a convenience store down the road. While he was gone, Lisa lit a fire and placed what candles she could find around the room. Then she dug through Will's nearly empty cabinets and came up with a bottle of wine. They ate on the floor beside the fire, feasting on roast beef sandwiches as if they were the choicest prime rib.

But Lisa chuckled as she snuggled into Will's velour robe and held out her hands to the fire's warming blaze. "Why is it that I never seem to get a decent meal out of you?"

Grinning, Will tugged his sweater off and settled on the silvery gray carpet beside her. Wearing only snug, faded jeans, zipped but not buttoned, he was a sight worth the sacrifice of many good dinners, but Lisa wasn't going to let him know that.

"You're always distracting me," she said, resisting as he pulled her close and nuzzled her neck.

"You really are on to me, aren't you?"

"You owe me something in lieu of a fancy supper."

"I have a few suggestions," he murmured, then whispered his erotic suggestion in her ear.

"Aren't you exhausted?"

"Are you?"

"I think I'd rather have some music."

"The piano's broken," he lied, and kissed her lips.

She pulled away. "No, it isn't. It's just covered in a thin layer of dust."

"So dust it."

"Play me something, Will, something that will help me remember tonight."

"Was tonight so special?"

She ran her hands up his bare arms, across his shoulders, down to the patch of dark hair in the center of his chest. His muscles were hard beneath her hands, but the look in his dark eyes was soft, so incredibly tender. Every night with him was special. Each moment she fell deeper in love with him. "Just play. Please. Just because I've asked you to."

"That's tough to turn down."

"Then play." She pushed him toward the black baby grand in the corner.

As he sat down, Lisa noticed the pictures missing from the wall behind him. Pictures of Mickey, she thought sadly. Gone, except for the yellowed wall that surrounded the vacant squares where they used to hang. Gone, like the man, but with their imprint still intact.

Will ran his hands over the piano keys. "What do you want? Slow or fast?"

Her gaze still on those empty spaces on the wall, Lisa said, "You choose."

He started with something light and effervescent. A classical piece that Lisa didn't recognize. But she smiled, letting the melody lift her and chase away any trace of sadness. Will was grinning, too, taking pleasure in the music. Lisa hugged her knees to her chest, momentarily content. Then the tempo shifted, and the words to a familiar Beatles song drummed in her head. A song about everyone's life, about loss, about the places and the people who had changed and passed on and away.

Lisa watched Will's face as he played. She knew the words to this song were running through his head, too. She saw the shadows that claimed his pleasure. It was so easy to slip, she realized. Every two steps that he took toward putting his pain in perspective were matched with a step backward. It snuck up on him, crept around corners. He could hide, he could pretend, he could refuse to "muddy things up," but there was little he could do to escape.

As the final chords faded, she went to him, took his hand, and together they went to the one place where she knew the shadows couldn't reach.

Later, Will held her while she slept, and sometime before dawn he realized what he wanted from Lisa.

Just love.

Only her love.

Somewhere out there in a nebulous, rosy-tinted future, he would tell Lisa how he felt. They would make a commitment. He would become Terry's father in every sense of the word. Maybe they would have more children. Awash in those dreams, Will fell asleep.

But reality was waiting for him. The next afternoon, the phone rang at Lisa's. Will answered, and the caller hung up.

It happened again that night.

And again the next morning.

Enraged by the reminder of the problems still facing them, Will threw the receiver across the kitchen. It hit against the wall and bounced on the floor.

At the table, where she sat drinking coffee, Lisa stared at him.

"That's it," he muttered. "Someone's going to do something about this."

"It's probably a prank, Will, that's all."

"And what about Terry? What if they—whoever *they* are—really did call him, pretending to be Rich? If Terry had been down here, he would have grabbed the phone, you know."

He watched the muscles work in her throat as she swallowed.

"That puts a whole new spin on it, doesn't it?"

"You're right. I'm calling the phone company—"

"No," he cut in, eyes narrowing. "You just leave this to me."

Chapter Nine

The late afternoon sun slanted through the standard, government-issue office blinds, highlighting Andy's concerned expression. "God help us, Will, what are you going to do next? Punch out everyone on the I.A. panel?"

The idea appealed to Will, who had just spent a frustrating hour with the officer in charge of that department. Then he had come to vent his anger with Andy, who was being almost as stubborn. "I just wanted Lt. Sherwood to know what's been going on."

"So you charged into his office unannounced and demanded that he do something about the calls Lisa has been getting."

"How do you know what I said?"

"I know you." The springs in Andy's chair squeaked as he leaned back. "And I know you're still about as edgy as you were before you got yourself suspended."

"Maybe I have reason to be edgy."

"But that's no reason to get yourself in more trouble than you already are."

Will studied his friend through narrowed eyes. "Am I in trouble, Andy?"

"You're suspended, for God's sake."

"I mean, what's the I.A. trying to pin on me?"

Andy's gaze didn't waver from Will's. "Why would I know if—and that's a big *if*—I.A. was trying to pin anything on you? I'm out of that department."

Glancing over his shoulder at the nearly empty Homicide office, Will lowered his voice. "I think you know a whole lot more than you've told me and Lisa."

"That's crap, and you know it."

"I know you," Will said, sarcastically repeating what Andy had said to him. "And I don't think you walked away from that investigation without an argument."

"Of course I didn't. I started the job. I wanted to see it through. But no one else saw it that way. So I'm back in Homicide." He tapped the stack of file folders on the corner of his desk. "Here's my present caseload to prove it."

"Would you tell me any different?"

"What do you think?"

"I asked you."

Muttering a simple but direct Anglo-Saxon word, Andy pulled his chair up to his desk. "Why don't you get out of here, Espinoza. I'm busy. I don't have time for your self-pitying crap today."

"What's that supposed to mean?"

"It means..." Andy began angrily, then took a deep breath. "It means you should know who your friends are."

Will's laugh was bitter. "Remember me, *amigo,* I'm the guy who got duped by his own uncle. You're asking me to trust anyone?"

"Yeah, I am. I think you should trust me. And I also think you should see a shrink about that mush you've got floating around in your brain."

"I don't need a shrink."

"You need something," Andy snapped. "I can't believe you. First you come tearing in, making demands to I.A. about those calls to Lisa—"

"So you think they're nothing?"

"I don't know what they are. But have you stopped to consider why Lisa would be targeted by Mickey's cronies and not you or me?"

"Because she got the dirt on him. She's the one who interviewed that hooker Mickey murdered." Hands on his hips, Will scowled at Andy. "Man, you're the one who warned Lisa to watch out."

"Because I knew things could get crazy," Andy retorted. "I mean, look what happened to Mickey when he realized Lisa was on to him. He flipped out. Who's to know what his cohorts are thinking or what kind of irrational action they might take? When I mentioned that to you and Lisa, I was just thinking we'd all be smart to be cautious. After all, nobody knows who was working with Mickey—"

"Obviously," Will said dryly. "If somebody knew something, they could get this mess cleared up. That's why I came in today, to try and rattle some cages."

"If you think it's so simple, how come you and Lisa turned up nothing for the first five months you were on the case?"

Grunting in frustration, Will flung himself into the chair beside Andy's desk. "All right," he conceded. "So maybe I should just sit tight and let I.A. snoop around until they turn over the right rock. But in the meantime, someone's trying to get to Lisa."

Andy shook his head. "You don't know that for sure. All you've got is a series of hang-up calls. It could be anyone. Even Lisa says that. And you know it, too, Will. It's not like you to be jumping to conclusions like this."

Hands braced on his knees, Will sat forward, staring down at the stained gray-and-black tile floor. Andy was right, of course. If he were thinking clearly these days, he would have seen it for himself. "Okay, so the calls could be anyone."

"That's right. So now, why don't you go home, or go to Elena's, or go find Lisa. Go somewhere and sit tight until this ends."

"There you go again," Will muttered, straightening up to glare at him. "You keep telling me to sit tight. You sound like you know something."

Andy groaned. "Are we back to that again?"

"I swear to God, if you knew something about what the I.A. has dug up on me—"

"Who says they're digging?"

"They talked to the guys in Narcotics about my record."

"Pretty standard stuff, wouldn't you say? Personally, if I were still in charge of the investigation and they *didn't* check out someone as close to Mickey as you were, I'd be raising hell and kicking some butts."

Will could see his point, but he wasn't through. "What about my captain over on the west side. He was always following me around, watching what I did."

"I would have watched you, too. You should have been forced to take some time off instead of taking on a new assignment."

"I wanted to stay busy."

"Oh, yeah," Andy scoffed. "And so you report for your new job, all tight-jawed, looking like you'll fly apart if you're spoken to."

"I did my job."

"Yeah, but you had all the symptoms of a loose cannon. I don't blame Captain Marshall for following you around. It's just a pity he didn't realize how his other lieutenant was pushing you."

"Punching him gave me a great deal of satisfaction."

"Maybe so," Andy agreed. "But the point I'm trying to make is that you don't know for sure what I.A. is doing. They questioned you, me and Lisa. And all of us assumed we were under suspicion. But have they called us in again?"

"No, but—"

"Then why don't we all forget it?" Again Andy thumped the files on his desk. "I'm getting on with my job. Lisa is, too. None of us has anything to hide."

Will exhaled a long, frustrated breath. "That's what Lt. Sherwood said to me. After I had ranted and raved to him for a while, he just leaned back, crossed his hands on that big old belly of his and said, 'Espinoza, if you haven't done anything wrong, what are you so worried about?' Damn, but he looked so smug I wanted to choke him."

"But he's right. That's the reason I've been saying we all just have to sit tight."

"Yeah, yeah, yeah," Will muttered, slumping back in his chair. "You're right. All of you are right. I just wish I.A. would make some kind of announcement, say we're all good cops and that they made a mistake."

Andy laughed. "You know it doesn't work that way. They never said we were bad cops. All they did was ask us some questions."

"And had the whole place buzzing with rumors."

"The rumors followed Mickey's death. They didn't come from I.A."

"But they could put a stop to them by issuing a statement of some sort."

Thoughtfully Andy rocked back in his chair again. "Maybe they're using the rumors."

"What's that supposed to mean?"

"It's just that I'm thinking . . . oh, nothing."

"Come on, tell me."

But Andy made a dismissive gesture. "I'm just second-guessing Lt. Sherwood."

"More power to you, then," Will said, getting to his feet. He thought Andy's guesses were probably more on target than Sherwood's best-laid plans, but Will knew he couldn't push Andy for information. His former partner might have been known as a gung-ho hotshot at one time, but Will knew he didn't indulge in too much idle speculation, even to his friends.

Will glanced around the familiar Homicide office. For over a year he and Andy had worked here as partners. The decor was predominantly gray, probably a fitting choice considering the crimes focused on by the detectives working here. As usual, someone had tried to inject some Christmas cheer by erecting an old, metallic-green tree in the center of the room. With typical police humor, however, all of the tree's red ball decorations were marked with a skull and crossbones.

Chuckling at the sight, Will turned back to Andy. "Has anybody complained about the tree this year?"

"Some folks don't seem to understand that if we didn't laugh about what we do, we'd lose our minds."

"How true."

"Do you want to come back to Homicide after this mess is cleared up? There'll be a slot open soon, when Reynolds retires."

Will glanced around the room again. He had good memories of this assignment, but he wasn't sure about coming back. "I don't know." He looked at Andy and then said what was really on his mind, "I'm not sure if I even want to be a cop anymore."

Going very still, Andy stared at him. "What do you mean, not be a cop? What else is there?"

Will shrugged. Law enforcement was the only career he had ever considered.

"You can't let Mickey do this to you," Andy said quietly. "If you leave the force, he will have destroyed more than his own life. No matter what he did, you are a good cop, Will. You're needed around here.''

"I just don't feel the same way I used to about the job.''

"Maybe that's not all bad. Maybe it shouldn't be such a crusade.''

Will frowned. A crusade was exactly how he had always viewed the job. Now he was questioning those views, wondering if this was where he belonged. But he didn't really want to get into that with Andy right now. Summoning a grin, he said, "Do you think I'm too old to be a rock star? I have the piano. Maybe I could give Elton John some competition in his old age.''

"I wouldn't turn in my badge just yet," Andy said with a wry chuckle. He picked up a pen, opened the folder on the top of his stack. "Now why don't you go upstairs and bother Lisa for a while. All she's got to worry about is some nut who's burning churches. I've got real problems here.''

Will thought he had spent enough time in police headquarters for one day. No matter what Andy said, he still felt uncomfortable with the rumors, still thought he was the subject of much speculation. He started down the hall from Homicide, heading for the backstairs, hoping he could avoid seeing anyone who might approach him.

As his bad luck would have it, however, he opened the stairwell door and ran right into an officer he knew. The two of them had been through the academy together, had briefly served on the same downtown third-shift patrol. Will nodded, thinking he could just duck away.

But the lanky redhead would have none of that. He stuck out his hand. "How are you, Espinoza?"

Somewhat surprised by the friendly openness, Will shook his hand, and murmured, "I'm okay."

"I've been meaning to call you," the man said, his gaze very direct. "I'm real sorry about what happened with Mickey. I know you two were tight."

Will started backing away. "Yeah, well . . ."

"And I'm also sorry about all the crap that's going around. I want you to know that you've got some friends on the force, Espinoza. We were all shocked to hear that Mickey . . ." He paused, then plunged ahead. ". . . Well, we were just shocked. But most people know none of that had anything to do with you."

The forthright statement of trust left Will almost speechless. All he managed to stammer was "Thanks."

The officer slapped him on the shoulder and with a final "Hang in there," pushed through the door to the hall.

Will didn't move for a minute. Since Mickey's death, he had been concentrating so hard on the people who seemed to distrust him that he had ignored those who had reached out to him in friendship. Not just Andy and Lisa, but others who had tried to offer sympathy. Over on the west side, there had been other officers who had tried to be friendly. He had been filled with so much anger, however, that he hadn't been able to respond. Maybe it was time he tried a little harder.

Toward that end, he took the stairs up to the third-floor arson department. Lisa wasn't in, however. Her captain said she was down in the basement, at the force's indoor shooting range.

Every year in Georgia, law officers were required to prove their weapons expertise. Lisa had told Will just this morning that she needed some target practice since her proficiency test was scheduled after the first of the year.

The basement range wasn't large, and every lane appeared to be in use as Will entered the room. The noise from the blasting guns was almost overwhelming. Grabbing some headphones from a rack beside the door, Will went down the line, looking for Lisa in each cubicle. He found her at the end. Only she wasn't firing.

She stood, her automatic gripped in both hands in front of her. She stared down at the gun, her face an unreadable, pale mask.

Will stood silently by, watching her. He knew better than to reach out, to startle her in any way. He also knew exactly what was going through her head.

She looked up finally, looked at him, *through* him. Her blue eyes were dark, wide and tortured. Just as they had been the night Mickey tried to kill her, the night he took his own life while clutching Lisa to his side. Will's mouth went dry as he remembered, as he watched Lisa's struggle with her own memories.

Lisa stared at Will for a full minute, trying to balance the reality of where they were with the memory of a cold, windswept rooftop. With effort, she got hold of herself. With the earphone-muffled *boom* of firing guns echoing all around them, she faced Will's dark, concerned gaze.

Not missing a beat, she turned, targeted the human silhouette at the end of the firing lane and fired the six bullets remaining in her clip. She pressed a switch, and the target moved toward her, so that she could see how she'd done. Not bad, she thought, especially considering how she had lost it after firing five shots. Without glancing at Will, she loaded another eleven-shot clip, sent another target into place, and aimed her gun. Again the results were good.

Only then did she look at Will, her chin uptilted, daring him to betray by word or expression his concern or pity.

Voice raised to counter the noise, she nodded to the target and said, "Not bad, huh?"

Will nodded, and he remained behind her while Lisa went through two more clips. When Lisa had finished her practice, and they moved out into the hall, she spoke before he could. "I need to get down here more often, don't you—"

"I need to know what that was about back there," Will retorted in a low voice as he drew her to the side of the hall.

"What do you mean?"

"Don't play dumb."

"I don't know what you mean," she insisted, pulling her arm from his grasp. "I was taking target practice. That's all."

"Lisa—"

"What brings you here, anyway?" she interrupted in a bright tone. "Couldn't stay away from me?"

He studied her for a moment. Then, obviously realizing she wasn't going to discuss what had happened, he said, "I saw Sherwood."

"And?"

Will told her what the man had said, about his talk with Andy. He ended by repeating what Andy had mentioned about I.A. "using" the rumors.

Lisa frowned. "I don't see how or why."

"You know Andy. The wheels are turning in his head, but he's not saying much until he has it all figured out."

"I just hope he finally made you realize that those phone calls probably have nothing to do with any of this. It's just a coincidence that some prank caller has my number. The car I saw parked across the street was nothing, too, I imagine. I just let my imagination run away with me that night."

"Is that what you were doing in there?" Will asked, jerking his head toward the range. "Was your imagination taking over then?"

Lisa made an impatient sound. "You're the one whose imagination is out of control." She turned and walked toward the elevator. Over her shoulder, she said, "I'm ready to leave for the day. Let's go home."

Will didn't push her to talk about the incident on their ride to the third floor or during their walk to the parking lot. At home, they had no chance for a private conversation. Terry was in high spirits, keyed up over the fact that the next day was Christmas Eve.

Lisa liked seeing her son happy and responding so openly to Will. Time was healing their rift, she thought. After dinner, she curled up on the sofa and watched them shake every wrapped package under the tree in an attempt to guess what each contained. Terry's biggest present from Will was a pair of much too expensive basketball shoes. Will had wrapped them in a huge box, and Terry had no idea what it contained. Will was pretending to be no less curious about the gifts with his name on them.

"I don't know which of you is the bigger kid," Lisa told him when Terry had finally been packed off to bed.

"It was good to see him acting like his old self." Will dropped down onto the sofa beside her, one arm looping around her shoulders. "By the way, what is in that box that's marked from you to me?"

"Oh, no," she said, laughing. "You're not starting that nonsense with me. Come to bed, and I'll give you a much better present."

Later, they snuggled under the blankets. Lisa was tired, sated from their lovemaking, but she wasn't really sleepy. Neither was Will.

With slow, loving motions meant to soothe rather than arouse, he stroked his hand up her thigh. "You were quiet tonight."

"I was enjoying you and Terry."

"Sure that's all?"

She knew he was trying to discuss the momentary panic she had experienced at the range. But the incident was the same as her nightmares, just more of her continuing reaction to that night with Mickey. Will didn't need to hear that. To this date, they had never really discussed that night. They had been reeling from the aftershocks for six weeks, they had talked all around it, but they had never confronted the tragedy itself. Lisa wondered if they ever would.

Though Will was beginning to heal, she couldn't forget his brokenhearted anguish. She could recall all too vividly how he had looked the morning after he had been suspended from the force. Sitting alone, dejected and despairing, he had been a man without hope. Perhaps his hope was returning, but she wasn't ready to add to his burdens just yet. She would deal with her anxiety and panic by herself for now.

So she snuggled closer to him now. She put her head on his shoulder, breathed in his familiar clean scent, and answered his question. "The *only* reason I was quiet tonight is because you and Terry didn't give me a chance to get a word in edgewise."

She couldn't see his expression in the dark, but he dropped a kiss on her forehead. "You seem really tired, Lisa. Maybe you should take some time off."

"While some lunatic is torching churches?"

He sighed. "I guess you're right." He was silent for a moment. "Do you ever think about doing something else?"

"Sure."

"Really?"

"After I was shot, and Terry was so upset, I thought I should quit, get a regular job." She laughed. "Don't you remember, you're the one who helped talk me out of it."

"Oh yeah," he said, a rueful note in his voice. "I told you it would be a waste if you left the force."

"And most of the time I think you were right."

"What about the other times?"

"The other times I feel the same as you and just about every other cop. It's a tough job for lousy pay."

"That it is."

Turning on her side, she gently touched his face. "What's all this about, anyway?"

"I don't know," he said after a moment's pause. "I've just been thinking, reconsidering my life."

"Trying to decide if you're going to quit?"

He sucked in his breath. "I guess I'm not too subtle, am I?"

"Not very," she agreed. "I can't tell you what you should do, Will. I just know that now isn't the time to make a decision like this."

"You're right." He breathed out again. "It's strange, isn't it? After all the fuss I made about not needing time off, now I'm not looking forward to going back."

"That'll pass."

"Maybe, but what if it doesn't?" Will stared into the dark. "What if it's never the same as it was before?" He thought of what Andy had said to him today, about the job being a crusade. He told Lisa.

"It's not a crusade for everyone."

"But it was for me," Will murmured. "I see that now. All my life, I looked at being cop like it was a holy quest. The goal was truth and justice. There were heroes and there were villains. No in-betweens. I mean, I know how the system works. I know that after we bring the bad guys in, a bunch of lawyers get together, sift through some papers and then justice isn't always served. But at least we bring 'em in. We do our job." Thinking of Mickey, he closed his eyes. "At least most of us do our jobs."

Lisa's arms tightened around him. "A lot of people would be surprised to know what a wide-eyed idealist you really are, Lieutenant Espinoza."

He had to smile. "You think my hard-ass image would be tarnished?"

"Possibly. But I also think it would be a shame for one of the good guys to give up his quest."

"Maybe," he murmured. The clock on the bedside table clicked, and he turned to read the digital display. "It's late, and you have to work tomorrow. Instead of discussing life philosophies, we should be getting some rest."

Very soon, Lisa was asleep. Will held her, spoon-fashion, still puzzling over what they had been discussing, until he also fell into a light slumber.

Sometime later he was awakened by Lisa's voice. She was muttering something in her sleep, her tone agitated, even though the words made no sense to Will's sleep-fogged brain. She had pulled away from him while she slept, but when he reached for her now, she cried out, fought him. Her words were still garbled, her voice full of terror, and she resisted his attempts to quiet her. But eventually he was able to pull her close.

"It's okay," he soothed, holding her tight. "It's going to be okay, Lisa. I'm here. I won't let anyone hurt you."

He wasn't sure if she ever really woke up, but her sounds of terror soon dissolved to quiet tears. All he could do was hold her while she cried. Even when the tears were over, and her breathing had become deep and steady, Will continued to hold her.

He had been a fool. All these weeks while locked in his selfish misery, he hadn't seen that Lisa was grappling with her own anxiety. He remembered the night she had screamed when he knocked on the kitchen door. He had known then that she was nervous and jumpy, but instead of trying to help her, he had accepted her insistence that she was fine. But she wasn't. Any idiot could look at her and tell she was overly tired and stressed. Any idiot but him.

Today, at the range, he had seen her terror. He had felt it tonight. But those were accidents. Lisa had kept her true feelings well hidden. He had behaved like such a selfish jerk, had abused the trust and intimacy of their relationship to such an extent that she had felt she couldn't be honest with him.

He felt so damn helpless, so sad, as if he had lost the most precious gift anyone had ever given him.

Satisfied that Lisa was resting well, he slipped from the bed, pulled on his jeans and went into the living room.

Who was he kidding? he thought as he moved through the darkened room. He had tried to pretend that they could eventually forget what had happened, just forget it and go on. But that wasn't true. With his own blood, Mickey had permanently stained their lives.

Will was too dispirited to feel even the usual anger. All he felt was frustration and loss. Shoving a hand through his hair, he paced to one of the front windows. Moonlight streamed inside. He and Lisa had forgotten to pull the curtains when they went to bed.

Outside, there was a heavy frost. The yard gleamed white and pure under the full moon. Will reached for the cord to pull the curtain shut, then he paused, his gaze sharpening.

Across the street, a car was parked.

In front of the empty lot. In the same spot where Lisa had seen one before.

The frost that covered the ground wasn't on the car, so it hadn't been there long. Impatient with his suspicions, Will told himself it was a neighbor who had returned late from a holiday party. But then there was a flare of light in the car. A match strike? Someone was watching the house. Boldly. Sitting right out front. It certainly wasn't something any cop worth their badge would do. So that let out I.A.

But who in the hell was it?

Without pausing to think, Will crossed the room to the closet under the stairs. He retrieved his gun from the holster he had stored on a shelf far from Terry's reach. In the kitchen, he disengaged the burglar alarm and stole, barefoot and shirtless, out the back and across the neighbor's yard. He went around their house and, keeping low to the ground, crossed the street. Some shrubs on the edge of the vacant lot shielded him as he snuck closer. There was definitely someone in the car. A man, he thought.

But what was he doing out here?

Taking a deep breath, Will crouched at the rear of the car and moved around to the side, trying to be quiet, trying to stay out of the man's rearview mirror. Finally, when he couldn't stand it another minute, he took a chance on the door being unlocked. He wrenched it open and stuck his gun in the man's startled, gaping face.

"Merry Christmas," Will said. "You just admiring the neighborhood, or did you want something special?"

"I—I'm not bothering anyone," the man sputtered.

"Yeah, you are. You're bothering me." With the gun, Will gestured for him to get out of the car.

The man was tall and blond. Handsome and well-dressed. The car was a gray BMW.

Will enjoyed watching him squirm. "Are you ready to tell me what you're doing out here?"

The man nodded, began, "It's kind of silly—"

"Notice I'm not laughing. Now what brings you to our little circle?"

"It's my son. He lives over there."

Will followed the direction he pointed. His eyes widened. The muscles in his throat clenched. But he lowered the gun.

The man said, "I feel so stupid."

Will nodded. "Well, *Rich . . .*"

Rich Talbot fell back a step at the mention of his name.

"In my opinion, *Rich,*" Will continued, "you *are* pretty stupid."

Chapter Ten

Over the loudspeaker of the fast-food restaurant, a Christmas carol was playing. Outside, the morning sun was shining. On the table in front of Lisa, a cup of coffee was cooling. All her senses were in operating order. Yet she still couldn't believe she and Will were seated in a booth with Rich.

It wasn't that Rich had changed much in eight years. His hair was still thick and honey blond. He was still slender and tall. He still had a charming smile.

"I can't apologize enough," he was saying. It was perhaps the tenth time he had apologized in the ten minutes since he had walked in the door and sat down with them.

Though she had tried, Lisa hadn't been able to grasp exactly why Rich had been parked outside her house. When Will had awakened her this morning with the news, she had been shocked and incredulous. She had sent Terry to a friend's, called the number Rich had given Will and had set up this meeting. But even now, none of this seemed real.

"I want you to go through it again," she said to Rich. "What are you doing here?"

"I've moved back to Atlanta," he explained. "The company I was working for in Oregon folded about a year ago and then I moved to another, but—"

"I know all that," Lisa cut in. "I tried to track you down."

"Well, the second job didn't work out too well, either," Rich continued. "I was in good shape financially, so I decided to take some time off, do a little traveling, some thinking. And I had a chance to realize what I had given up with Terry. I couldn't get him off my mind."

"You managed to forget him pretty well for eight years."

"All that's changed. I came to Atlanta just before Thanksgiving and accepted a new job that'll start after the New Year. I had to go back to Oregon to clear up some personal business. But now I'm here. For good."

Rich's gaze met Lisa's, then skittered away. "I want to see Terry, Lisa."

"That's why you were sitting outside my house in the middle of the night? What were you thinking, that he was going to come out and play?"

Rich had the grace to look ashamed. "It was stupid, I know, but I haven't been sleeping well, and so a couple of times I've driven over and sat outside your place, thinking about what I've been missing for the past eight years."

"What were you going to tell the police if they cruised by?" Will asked.

"The truth, I guess," Rich admitted. "I didn't really think things through very well."

A major understatement, Lisa thought, shaking her head. Nothing about Rich had really changed. He never considered the consequences of his actions. "So you really did call Terry?"

"I'm sorry about that," Rich said, leaning forward. "I've called a couple of other times, too, but you always answered or a man did." He glanced at Will. "I suppose it was you."

"There isn't any other man answering my phone," Lisa interjected hotly.

"Okay, okay," Rich said, holding up his hands. "I wasn't implying anything. You have a right to a life."

"Well, thank you so much for your permission." Beneath the table, Will gently touched her leg, reminding her to be cool. As had been the case all morning long, Will had been holding her together.

She steadied herself, then continued. "Rich, I just don't understand why you kept calling and hanging up. If you wanted to see Terry, why didn't you just talk to me?"

Rich hung his head again. "I know what you think of me, Lisa. We may have only talked a half dozen times in the past eight years, but when we did, your contempt for me as a father rang through loud and clear. Every time I called, I started to talk to you. But I always lost my nerve."

"That was a pretty lousy trick," Will muttered. "You had us worried. You upset Terry."

"I'm sorry," Rich said yet again. "I know I shouldn't have talked to Terry, but when he answered . . . well, I couldn't resist. I've handled all this badly."

Lisa wanted to ask him why he couldn't write a letter, or have his lawyer get in touch, but she knew trying to follow Rich's reasoning was a process too complicated for her brain to perform right now. "Tell me why I should trust you to see Terry."

"Trust me?"

"Who's to say you won't run out on him again? He's not a baby now, Rich. This time, if you leave him, he won't get over it easily."

"I won't leave," Rich promised. He went on to explain that he had been through therapy, that he had come to realize that a job and its financial rewards weren't all there was to life. He wasn't going to go chasing a financial opportunity somewhere else. The company he would be working with in Atlanta had allowed him to write his own ticket. He would be here for a long time. That's what he wanted, years with Terry. He had seen friends with their children, and had come to see what he was missing. He painted quite a touching picture of how much he wanted to see his boy.

His boy. The man's proprietary tone set Will's teeth on edge. But as he listened to Rich, he thought he could understand why Lisa had married him. He talked a smooth game, was very convincing. The question was whether there was any substance behind his ingratiating smile.

Lisa's expression was as skeptical as Will's thoughts. He was glad she wasn't buying into her ex-husband's line. She interrupted his spiel, "Rich, I hope you'll understand why I'm reluctant to let you see Terry."

A frown drew Rich's eyebrows together. "It's because I hit you that time, isn't it?"

The words were like a sucker punch to Will's gut. "What?"

Rich was looking at Lisa, ignoring Will. "That was the only time I've ever hit anyone. I swear to you, Lisa—"

"You hit her?" Will interrupted again before Lisa could say anything more. Fury engulfed him.

"We had an argument about my quitting the force," Lisa explained in blunt terms. "Rich got out of control and slapped me. It was the final act in what had become a very bad marriage. I left him the next day."

Rich added, "I was young and immature, and I thought Lisa belonged at home with our child. It was a stupid thing to do."

Lisa's next words echoed Will's thoughts. "You've done a lot of stupid things, Rich."

"Does that mean I don't have a right to see our son?"

She paused. "I don't know."

"I have a legal right."

Eyes narrowing, Lisa sat forward. "Is that a threat of some sort? Because if it is, I don't know too many judges who would look kindly on a man who deserted his child for eight years."

"At least I supported him."

She laughed. "You think that money was all the support Terry needed? He wanted a father—"

"And I'm ready to be one."

"Oh, sure, now *you're* ready. And what about when you decide it's not all fun and games and father-son bonding—"

"You're twisting what I said earlier, Lisa—"

"Hey, hey," Will interrupted. "I don't know that arguments are getting either of you, or Terry, anywhere."

Rich slumped back in his seat. "You're right. I didn't come here to fight. I want to see our son, Lisa. I'm going to see him, one way or the other. It would be a lot easier if I have your support."

She looked down at the table. "I can't give you an answer right now."

"Tomorrow's Christmas, Lisa—"

"Yes," she said, looking up. "And *our* family, *Terry's* family has quite a nice day planned."

Rich's mouth tightened, but he didn't press. "I'd appreciate hearing from you soon, Lisa." Nodding to Will, he stood and left the restaurant.

"What am I going to do?" Lisa murmured.

Will took her hand. "Do you think he would ever hurt Terry?"

"If you mean hit him, I don't think so. Surprisingly enough, I believe Rich when he says that was an isolated incident. I think he was always threatened by my independence and my job. Finally, he just had it with being married to me, being married in general."

"What about when he's had it with being a father?"

She bit her lip. "Physical harm isn't what I'm afraid of. I don't trust him to stick around. I can't take that kind of chance with Terry's feelings."

Will squeezed her fingers. "I don't know if you have a choice, Lisa. Legally I'm not sure he can be barred from seeing his son. And if Terry ever found out you tried to keep his father away..."

"Oh, God," she whispered. "He'd never forgive me."

"I think you're going to have to try to trust Rich."

She gave him a wan smile. "Quite a merry Christmas, isn't it?"

He put his arm around her shoulders. "We'll survive."

They did more than just survive, of course. There were some bright points Will knew he would remember. Terry racing downstairs at five in the morning to open his gifts. His face when he opened the shoes from Will. Watching Lisa's eyes light up at the leather boots Will gave her. Unwrapping his own gifts. A tie rack Terry had made for him at the Y. And from Lisa, a complete collection of Jerry Lee Lewis's best recordings on CD.

They made breakfast together, all three of them. Thick pancakes dripping with butter and syrup with sausage on the side. It felt good, laughing together, cleaning up the discarded paper and bows, playing with Terry's new gadgets. It felt like a family. They were a family, just as Lisa had told Rich yesterday.

Will thought himself lucky. He did his best not to think of other Christmases with Mickey.

That was more difficult when they went to Elena's for lunch and more gifts. The day was hard for her. Will saw the strain in her eyes, heard it in her forced laughter. But she persevered, as always. Unlike Thanksgiving, when Mickey's ghost had waited in every corner for Will, this day was much easier. He didn't indulge in any fond reminiscing. He wasn't sure he would ever be able to recall the good times with Mickey.

The saddest part was knowing this was the last Christmas Elena would spend in this house, Will's childhood home. Though no offer had been made on the property as of yet, there were some good prospects. And it was a foregone conclusion that the house would be sold. Since being suspended, Will had had the time to go over Elena's finances again and again. She *had* to sell.

Just before they left, Elena gave Lisa a final gift, the Christmas angel she hadn't been able to put on her own tree.

When Lisa protested, Elena said, "It's special to me. But I won't ever use it again. It will give me more pleasure knowing it's on your tree next year."

While Lisa and Terry went to say goodbye to Marta, Will knelt beside Elena's wheelchair. He took one of her hands in his. He tried his damnedest to think of the words that would show her how much he loved her. But none came.

Gently she brushed the hair from his forehead, exactly as she had done when he was Terry's age. "I know," she whispered. "I know what's in your heart."

Her smile was brilliant, ethereal. "Now, go. Go home with Terry and Lisa."

Home. Once upon a time, that one sweet word had brought images of this house. Will knew a part of his heart would remain here forever. But his home was really wherever Lisa and Terry were.

At home, however, Lisa had to tell Terry about Rich.

She had imagined telling him would be difficult. It wasn't. The hard part came when she had to call Rich, had to hand Terry the phone so he could talk to his father. The hard part was when Rich came over, his arms loaded with expensive gifts. The hard part was sitting in the kitchen with Will while her son visited with the father who had deserted him.

Terry took everything in stride. He didn't greet Rich with open arms, but he wasn't reticent, either. And he was so happy. Lisa couldn't help but respond to that happiness.

That night, when Rich was gone and Terry was finally in bed, Lisa and Will went up to say a last goodnight. Tired as the boy had to be, he was still awake, holding the remote-control plane Rich had brought him.

He smiled sleepily up at Lisa. "It was the best Christmas ever, Mom."

She took the plane away, and tucked the covers in around him. "I'm glad you're happy, son."

"I am. I got my dad back."

Standing in the doorway, Will told himself it was small of him to feel even a twinge of jealousy. As a boy, he had often wished for his father. He understood Terry's feelings.

Yet he stood there, feeling like an outsider. Just this morning, he and Lisa and Terry had been a family. Now that was changed. Will couldn't help thinking that if he hadn't drifted away from Terry after Mickey's death, he wouldn't feel so insecure, so shut out. The sensation ended the holiday on a discordant note.

That note lingered the next day, vibrated through the week that followed.

Terry wanted to be with his father as much as possible. At first, Lisa only allowed Rich to visit him at home. But eventually he wanted to spend some time with Terry alone. Lisa gave in on New Year's Day. She was a nervous wreck the entire day, walking the floor, jumping at the sound of the phone or a car outside.

Will tried to distract her, tried to get her to talk about her feelings. But she wouldn't open up. The closeness they had once known was altered, damaged. He'd known that since the night Rich had showed up outside the house.

He blamed Mickey for opening this chasm between himself and Lisa. But he blamed himself for being unable to bridge it. He and Lisa were like familiar strangers, living together, going through the motions of everyday life, but without interacting on any significant level. Even the passion that had sustained them in the last few weeks wasn't enough.

Will fell into a dark depression, blacker perhaps than the rage that had gripped him after Mickey's death.

Lisa just concentrated on coping.

Terry was her major concern. She wanted to believe Rich was ready to be the father their son needed. She even allowed herself to hope. But she didn't burden

Will with long, pointless discussions of her doubts and fears. Only weeks ago, he had been buckling under the pressures of his own life. He might have regained some of his strength, but the pressures were still there. Elena. He was asking profound questions about his career. Instead of returning to work after New Year's, Will had requested another month in vacation time off. Lisa could see how troubled he was. She didn't want to add to his concerns.

Right now her life felt like a house of cards, teetering, almost ready to crash. But it wasn't Will's responsibility to hold her up.

Even on the job, she was off balance. She followed one dead-end lead after another in the church arsons, while struggling to keep up with her other cases. Sometimes she felt like a rookie again, a female in a man's world, as if she needed to prove how tough she was.

One night about two weeks into January, Lisa allowed Terry to spend the night with Rich. She had run out of excuses not to let him go. Rich had been holding up his part of the bargain, so, reluctantly, she gave in to Terry's pleas.

She and Will made a feeble stab at a romantic dinner. But her heart wasn't in the evening. Finally they went to bed early, and she fell into an exhausted sleep.

The phone jarred her awake sometime later. Her first disjointed thoughts were of Terry. She grabbed the receiver while Will snapped on the bedside lamp.

But it was her boss on the other end of the line, not Terry. Tersely he said, "There's a church on fire right now." He gave the address. "Get down there and see what you can come up with."

Will came with her. Lisa protested, but while she dressed, he pulled on jeans and a sweater and strapped on his gun. They rode in silence through the city.

It was warm for January, one of those damp, dreary nights that came so often to the southeast in the winter. The day's rain had changed to a mist that did nothing to curb the inferno that raged on a street corner in south Atlanta.

The church was an old structure, wooden, with a steeple that soared high above the flames below. Firemen were hard at work, trying to save the building. But it looked like a lost cause. All they could hope for was to keep it from spreading to the houses nearby. Even that looked doubtful.

Beyond the flashing lights, the shouts of firemen, the suffocating smoke and the tangled coils of hose, members of the community stood, their shocked and shaken faces lit by the blaze that split the night sky.

It was into the crowd that Lisa went. To a gray-haired woman who was clutching a pair of bronzed baby shoes to her chest as she prayed her house wouldn't go. To the soot-streaked and anguished young minister who had made a wild, reckless dash from his parsonage into the church to try to save the silver offering plates and a Bible that had belonged to his father. To the teenage punks who joked about roasting marshmallows and seemed to think the whole thing was one big bonfire.

To each of them, Lisa went with her questions. *Had they seen anyone, anytime, who acted suspiciously?*

Any strangers in the neighborhood? Anyone with a grudge against the pastor or the church community?

Over and over again, she got the same negative responses. Finally, frustrated, she sat down on the bumper of a car and watched the church burn.

Will came and sat down beside her. "Anything?"

She shook her head, recounted what she knew. "There was an explosion. The windows blew out. The flames started. It fits the pattern of the other fires. Middle of the night. Sudden. Seemingly for no reason."

"The house beside it lost its roof," Will muttered.

Thinking of the older woman with her baby shoes and her lost expression, Lisa slumped back against the car. Again she scanned the crowd. In the smoke and the haze, a face peered out at her, teased her memory, then disappeared. Lisa frowned, realization hit, and she was on her feet, pushing through the clutch of frightened people.

When she reached the far side, she saw a shadow slip between two houses. She quickened her pace. The slender man she followed looked over his shoulder and began to run.

"Police," Lisa yelled, her voice blending with the noise of the fire scene. "Stop where you are!" She bent, slipped her gun from her ankle holster and yelled again.

But the man didn't stop.

There wasn't time to consider her actions, no time to call for backup. She followed as he turned down the alley behind a row of houses. They dodged garbage cans and household debris. In the dim light, the man flashed in and out of Lisa's sight. She kept yelling for him to stop. He didn't. But she gained on him. Behind her there were other pounding footsteps. She heard Will call her name. But it was the man ahead who claimed Lisa's attention. He was just ahead, almost close enough to touch, but he wouldn't stop. At the end of the alley, he wheeled to face her, and something glinted in his hand. A gun? It didn't matter. Lisa was too close, moving too fast. She plowed into him, dragged him to the ground. They rolled over damp, cool earth and against a wire-mesh fence.

When the struggle was over, Lisa was in control, with her gun at the man's throat. Beside the man was an aluminum flashlight, the glint she had seen in the dark.

Will slid to a stop beside them, dropped down to hold the man as Lisa got to her feet. In the light that streamed from the back porch of a nearby house, the man, who was sobbing now, was clearly visible.

He was young, mid-thirties, a convicted arsonist released from prison several years ago, supposedly living in a small town south of Atlanta with his mother, supposedly rehabilitated. His photo and name had been on the list they had checked out when these church fires began, but he seemed like a long shot. Only when Lisa had seen his face in the crowd had everything clicked in her head. In years past, he had a fondness for torching schools in the middle of the night. His target had shifted to another institution. But he still liked to be in the crowd to watch them burn. That was part of his sickness.

"I'm sorry," he sobbed now, looking up at Lisa. "Tell Mama I'm sorry."

Calmly, Lisa listened as he confessed to this arson and others.

She rode that emotionless high all through the night. She and Will took the man in, booked him and called her captain to give him the news. Despite being up half the night, she and Will were both wide awake, so they went up to her office to do their reports. By that time it was early morning.

Will and Lisa rode down the elevator, only to find that the front lobby was filled with media. Newsmen, reacting to the outrage of the public, had given high visibility to the church fires. Lisa assumed they were out in force to capture the story of the arsonist's arrest. There had been a photographer at the fire last night. Lisa could remember his flash going off in her face as she and Will had followed the handcuffed suspect and a uniformed officer through the crowd. She supposed he had leaked the man's capture.

Now the police department's public-relations spokesperson was in front of the media crowd, trying to field questions. Will and Lisa ducked out a side door and went home.

Silently, Lisa showered, slipped on her robe, went to the kitchen for coffee. Will, though he looked at her with concern, said nothing before he went to take his own shower.

When he was gone from the room, Lisa's calm shattered. Reaction set in. Shaking, she sank down in a chair at the dining table.

Will found her there sometime later, white-faced and trembling.

"Oh, Lisa," he murmured, and tried to put his arm around her shoulders.

She held him off, and managed a broken, "No."

"But you're shaking, Lisa. You're frightened."

"No, I'm not," she denied, her voice gaining strength. "I'm just tired."

"Lisa—"

"I'm okay."

"You just chased a man, tackled him, not knowing if he had a weapon or not. Then you stayed up all night. I'd say you're not okay."

"I did a job, all right. That's all it was. And I'm fine with it. I'm just fine."

"No, you're—"

"Damn it, Will, just leave me alone."

He drew back, startled.

She closed her eyes, sucked in a deep, shuddering breath, and repeated, "Just leave me alone."

The words summarized everything that was wrong between them, Will realized. Despite the passion that they had shared. Despite all their efforts to put their relationship back on an even keel. Despite it all, they weren't really together. Lisa didn't trust him enough to accept simple human comfort from him.

But why should she trust him? He had been disappointing her in big and small ways ever since Mickey died. Hell, he had let her down long before that awful November night. If he had read the warning signs in Mickey's behavior, Lisa would have never been in danger. If she had trusted him as her partner, she would have told him her suspicions about Mickey. If she trusted him now...

But she didn't. And Will didn't blame her. After all, why should anyone trust Mickey Vallejo's nephew? The circle always came back to Mickey. Always would, Will feared.

The doorbell rang then, a strident sound in the silent sun-washed kitchen. Dragging a hand through her still-damp hair, Lisa brushed past Will on her way to the front door.

Will stood ramrod still until Andy's voice penetrated his thoughts. He turned just as Lisa led their friend into the kitchen.

Andy's gaze met his. "It's hit the fan, Will."

"What are you talking about?"

"The I.A. investigation," Andy retorted. "The indictments are being handed down right now. I understand the grand jury was in session all night."

Startled, Lisa's gaze flew to Will's. She realized now that the media hadn't been out on a Sunday morning because of an arsonist, however heinous his crimes.

Andy's next words confirmed her thoughts. "Tomorrow it'll be front-page news."

Chapter Eleven

Law enforcement was more than a career. Police officers were more that co-workers. It was a brotherhood, a sisterhood. A family circle. Inside that circle, they might chastise their own. But the circle remained tight. They guarded their secrets, often hid their shame.

This time, however, the circle didn't hold.

When Andy called the I.A. investigation front-page news, he was being conservative. Lisa could only invoke a cliché to describe what ensued during the next week. It was a media circus.

Mickey's murder of a hooker, his suicide and the hint that he had been on the take, had rated only a mention in the newspapers back in November. Now it was the lead story at six and eleven. It was picked up by every newspaper in the region. Lisa even got a call from one of the sleazy national TV tabloid shows.

She couldn't blame the journalists, of course. It was a story made to sell newspapers, made for television. The blond cop gets the dirt on her policeman lover's uncle, who is also a cop. A cop loved by everyone, including his long-suffering, invalid wife. The uncle kills himself. But there are questions about how and why he died. Was there a lover's triangle? No, just corruption, a tangle of graft that stretched to every level of the police department.

Murder, passion and madness. This story had it all, Lisa thought. And the press exploited every angle.

After only a week, Lisa had become sick of seeing the picture of her and Will that had been snapped the night of the church fire. In the photo, she was disheveled, her jeans and sweater covered in dirt, her hair wild around her shoulders, her eyes wide. With his face unshaven, his own hair mussed and his leather jacket askew, Will looked rough, dark and dangerous. Several inventive reports made much of their appearance.

She and Will and Elena weren't the only ones to suffer, of course. There were all those people that I.A. had indicted. Lisa had to hand it to Internal Affairs. They had done their jobs well. While everyone in the department had been wondering about Will, I.A. had quietly continued with an investigation they had been working on for a year. Mickey was only a part of a large-scale inside operation that had been taking money from criminals and ordinary citizens alike for a long time. Fifteen police officers would be tried for the betrayal of their badges.

On the Sunday a week after the storm hit, Lisa sat alone in her kitchen. Terry was upstairs, waiting for

Rich to come and get him. At school, a lot of her son's friends, no doubt egged on by their parents, had asked him about the news reports. He had been full of questions about Mickey. She had tried to be as honest as she could. On Friday afternoon, he had come home upset, a scratch on his cheek from a fight over something one of the other boys had said about Lisa.

She just wanted it to be over. All of it.

Then she and Will would...what? she thought. What about she and Will? He had retreated into himself again. Lisa knew she had herself to blame for that. At least in part. God, she wished she could go back a week, to that moment here in the kitchen when Will had tried to comfort her. Why had she pushed him away? Why had it seemed so important that she be strong? Maybe it had been habit. She had gotten so used to hiding her true emotions from him that she hadn't known when to stop. So many times during the past week she had wanted Will's comfort. But he hadn't offered it again. He hadn't even been here.

The doorbell rang, just as it had last Sunday. Lisa didn't move, knowing her son would race to meet his father. Rich was early, but that was fine, considering the occasion. Terry's birthday was this Wednesday. Rich had been out of town on business for part of the week, but he was coming over today to take Terry and some friends to an arcade and out for pizza. Lisa had wondered if the day should go ahead as planned, given the problems Terry had had with some of the boys. But it was probably best that they all return to normal. They couldn't hide out in the house forever.

She listened as Terry bounded down the stairs and opened the door, but it was Will's voice that greeted him. Heart leaping with hope, she got up and went into the living room.

He looked almost as grim and dangerous as he had in that newspaper photo, with hollows under his eyes and lines around his mouth. He stood by the door, half answering Terry's questions while his gaze was on Lisa.

Terry's voice cut into Lisa's thoughts. "Will, can you tell me?"

Will looked down at the boy, as if only then realizing he was there. Eyes softening, he laid a hand on Terry's shoulder. "Tell you what, *amigo?*"

"What Mickey did that was wrong."

The shutters dropped back into place in Will's expression.

"Oh, Terry," Lisa murmured, coming forward. "We've talked about this and talked about it. You know what he did."

"But I don't understand."

Lisa didn't normally brush Terry's questions aside with the sort of answers her parents' generation might have given. But she did this time. "You'll understand when you're older," she told him. "Now go upstairs and wait for your father."

"But I want to talk to Will," Terry insisted petulantly. "Where you been, Will? I got in a fight at school. I wanted to to tell you about it, but Mom—" he darted a resentful glance at Lisa "—wouldn't let me. See the scratch I got?"

Lightly, Will put a finger to the thin red line on his cheek. "What was the fight about?"

"Bruce called Mom a name, that name you told me not to call girls. He said his dad said she was a pretty little—"

"That's okay," Will interrupted before Terry could explain. "I get the picture. Did you beat him up?"

"Sort of."

"Well, it's a good scratch, anyway."

Terry looked pleased, but he returned to his original question. "Explain about Mickey, okay?"

Lisa stepped forward then, grasping her son's shoulders. She turned him firmly toward the stairs. "March, young man. I already told you we're not talking about Mickey. Now, go."

Halfway up the stairs Terry turned, his face red, eyes brimming with tears. "Why are you being so mean, Mom? I don't understand why it's wrong to talk about him. Will told me I could talk to him about anything. Why not about Mickey?"

"Because I said so," Lisa retorted.

Fighting his tears, Terry fled upstairs. In a few seconds the windows shook from the force of his slammed door.

"I'm sorry," Will said.

Lisa whirled to face him. She was so tired of hearing those words from him. "What are you sorry for?"

"For all of this."

"Oh, please, Will—"

"No," he said, stepping forward. "You're going to listen to me, Lisa." He took a deep breath. "I am sorry. Sorry that you got dragged into this mess."

"No one dragged me anywhere."

"Didn't Mickey drag you up on that roof?"

"Will—"

"Ever since that night nothing has been right."

"Only because you won't let it be right. Because you won't accept it and go on."

Will took hold of her shoulders. "Have you accepted it, Lisa? Is it acceptance that gives you nightmares? That leaves you shaking when you look at a gun? Does acceptance have you nervous and jumpy and frightened?"

She lifted her chin. "I can deal with those things."

He paused, his eyes scanned her face. "Well, I can't."

Lisa swallowed. "What are you saying?"

"That I'm ending it. It's over. I'm getting out of your life. After this past week, I know this is the only thing I can do. The only way this nightmare is going to end is if I get out of your and Terry's lives and stay out. That way Mickey will stay dead and buried and forgotten. And you can put this behind you at last."

She was silent for a moment. Then her next words struck Will like blows. "So you're going to take the coward's way out?"

"The only way."

"Mickey's way."

He sucked in his breath.

"He didn't want to face facts so he put a gun to his head." Lisa's gaze didn't waver from Will's. "And now, instead of staying here with me, working this out, you're going to leave, too." Her laugh was bitter. "I guess Mickey really did teach you a thing or two, didn't he?"

The comparison was like a spear digging into Will's insides. "This isn't like Mickey," he forced out. "Don't you see, Lisa, you're right. I can't put what Mickey did behind me. I thought I could. I came to you and I tried. But I failed. And because of that, I can't be what you and Terry need. I'm not . . ." He paused, put a hand to his heart. "I'm just not whole, anymore. And you deserve more than that."

Lisa steadied herself by taking hold of the stair railing. "It seems that you've thought this through very well."

"I know that I've already hurt you enough. Hell, Lisa, you don't even trust me anymore."

"I don't trust you?" she repeated slowly.

"No."

"You've got it all wrong, Will. You've had it wrong from the beginning."

He put his hand on the doorknob. "In a few days, when you've had time to think it over, I believe you'll see that this is the right thing to do."

Anger flooded through her as she watched him open the door. So he knew what was right for them, did he? Well, far be it from her to burst his bubble. "All right," she said. "Just go. Get out of here. What we had . . ." She managed a tight, little laugh. " . . . What we had ended that night with Mickey. You haven't been the same since then. You aren't the man I thought you were."

His eyes were deep, welling pools of misery.

She wanted him to hurt. She wanted to hurt him as he was hurting her. "No, you aren't the man I thought I loved. You're much more like Mickey."

She didn't wait to see the devastation that statement would bring to him. She turned and walked away. And in a few minutes the door closed softly.

Lisa wanted to run away somewhere, to hide her head under a pillow. She settled for sitting down at the kitchen table to cry.

Terry came down sometime after Will had left. He stood in the kitchen doorway and stared at her. "Did Will make you cry, Mom?"

She wiped the tears from her cheeks. "No, Terry. I made myself cry."

"I heard you fighting."

"I'm sorry."

"Is Will ever coming back?"

She didn't sugarcoat the bad news. "Maybe not, son."

Terry looked as if he was going to cry, too.

She took a deep breath. She needed to hold herself together for her son. "It'll be okay, Terry. I'm here for you. And you've got your dad..." Her words trailed away as she glanced at the kitchen clock. Where was Rich, anyway?

"What time is your dad supposed to be here?" she asked Terry.

"One-thirty." Terry glanced at the clock, too. He turned panicked eyes to Lisa. "It's almost two. Where is he?"

"Don't worry. He must be stuck in traffic."

At two-thirty, he still wasn't there. He didn't answer his phone. And Terry was frantic. Lisa offered to take him and his friends out, but he didn't want that. Part of the novelty about the day was going to be showing off his father. Terry's face had the adult, disappointed look Lisa knew all too well. Instead of crying and raging, he just went upstairs. He wouldn't even come down to eat.

Lisa did the raging. She called Rich's apartment until midnight, until he finally answered. His business trip had run long. He had forgotten about Terry's party.

"You can't do this," Lisa stormed at him.

"I'm sorry," Rich kept saying. "I just forgot. I'm not used to having to think about someone else."

You do this again, and you won't see him anymore, do you understand?"

"Put him on the phone. I'll explain."

"It's midnight, for God's sake. He's asleep. You can do your apologizing some other time."

"Lisa, I'm sorry—"

She slammed down the phone on the last word. She'd had her fill of men apologizing today.

Still fuming, Lisa went to her room, threw herself on the bed. She felt as if everyone in her life had betrayed her.

She just kept letting it happen. She let Rich waltz into Terry's life. Against her better judgment she had begun to trust him. And now look what had happened.

As for Will…even after she had decided she wanted more from him than he could give, even after she knew she wanted his love, she had settled for less. She let herself be tempted by what little he could offer. And now he was gone. Damn it, it wasn't fair. She had been there for him these last few months. Again and again, she had set aside her own needs, her own anxieties.

And for what? For him to say she didn't trust him, that they were better off apart. She had to accept—

She sat up on her bed. Why did she have to accept any of what Will had said? One by one, the realizations began to tick through Lisa's head.

Month's ago, Elena had told her not to coddle Will. But Lisa had gone ahead, hiding her feelings from him, trying to protect him. On one hand, she had been demanding that he accept the facts about Mickey. At the same time, she had been trying to hide her own residual fear and terror over Mickey's attempt on her life. That reaction had become instinctive, until last Sunday when she had pushed away Will's attempt to comfort her. Why? she asked herself again, Why had she done that? She should have listened to the advice people had given her. Everyone had told her to be honest about her own feelings—the psychologist, Elena, even Meg on that afternoon in the park.

But Lisa hadn't been honest with Will. And from the beginning of their relationship, when they had become friends, they had been honest. Honest, open and direct. Why hadn't Lisa remained true to herself? If she had been honest with Will, he wouldn't now believe she didn't trust him.

Of course, Will hadn't been honest with her, either. Or had he? Ever since his uncle's death, he had said he was too filled with anger at Mickey to feel much of anything else. And Lisa, in her direct way, had kept pushing at him to lose the anger, to get on with the grieving and healing. And he had begun to heal. In the last few weeks, he wasn't so angry all the time. He had even brought Mickey into the conversation once in a while. But she had ignored all that. She had been too impatient with him. Dr. Hastings, Andy, Elena—all of them had urged her to give him time.

She hadn't, however. She had pushed him away and out the door. She had said terrible, hurtful things to him. Things she didn't mean. And now he was gone.

But it didn't have to stay that way.

Tomorrow, she thought, lying back on the pillows. Tomorrow, she would go to Will. They would work this out. She loved him. That should be all that mattered.

With her mind more settled than it had been in weeks, Lisa fell into a deep dreamless sleep.

She woke to the sound of the telephone. The ringing made her sit straight up and look around with blinking eyes. A glance at her clock told her it was almost nine o'clock. She was late for work. Terry was late for school. Lisa's brain kicked into overdrive as she snatched up the phone.

It was Elena. "Lisa, I thought you should know that Terry is on his way here."

Lisa blinked again. "What?"

"He called here from a pay phone. He was very upset. Will's gone to pick him up."

"I'll be right there." Lisa looked around the room again wondering how long Terry had been gone.

Will pulled his car to a stop at the small residential park near Elena's house. He turned to face the unhappy young boy beside him. Terry had said very little after Will located him at a shopping mall near his school. Under pressure, he had explained that he had gotten up this morning, without disturbing his mother, caught the school bus and then walked to the mall instead of going to school. He had thought this running-away business out very carefully.

Cutting the engine, Will said, "Okay, *amigo,* now you can tell me what this is all about."

"I want to go to Elena's. Maybe she'll talk to me. Mom's upset all the time. Dad forgot my party yesterday. And you left. I thought maybe Elena would talk. She's always so nice to me."

Unlike the other adults in his life, Will thought guiltily. "I'll talk to you, Terry."

"You wouldn't yesterday."

"It wasn't a good time."

"Because you were going to fight with Mom?"

Will sighed. It was too much to hope that anything would escape Terry's notice. "Yeah," he said finally. "I had to fight with your mom."

"You broke up?"

Smiling at the very adult phrase, Will nodded.

Terry exhaled. "I just don't know why everything has to be so messed up. It's all Mickey's fault."

"I think you're right about that."

There was a pause, then a tentative, "Do you hate Mickey?"

Again, Will nodded.

"I tried to," Terry said, his brow wrinkling in concentration. "But I couldn't. I kept doing what you told me to do."

"What's that?"

"I thought about the good stuff about him."

Clearly, Will remembered the night in Terry's room when he had given the boy that advice. Advice he couldn't take himself.

"I tried to hate you, too," Terry went on quickly. "And Dad, too. But I couldn't do that, either. I mean, you do stuff I don't understand, but I still love you. Mom says that's what you do. She says she'd love me no matter what I did. Couldn't you do that with Mickey?"

Will felt as if a hammer had split open his skull. This little boy had sat here and with such perfect logic, spelled out what Will had been grappling with for months. Even when people did wrong, you still loved them.

Even when they were as wrong as Mickey.

Real people weren't either heroes or villains. Everyone had the potential for good and bad. It was a lesson Will should have learned long ago.

He sat in stunned silence as Terry continued. "Dad really made me mad by not showing up yesterday, but that doesn't mean I don't want to see him again. I was mad at you, too, for a long time, but I want to see you, too.

"I'm glad about that," Will said. Yesterday, when he had walked away from Lisa, he had known he was giving Terry up, too. And that had hurt. The boy was important to him. "I guess the thing you have to remember is that we grown-ups make mistakes. We're not perfect. We're just men and women."

"I know that," Terry said, sounding as if Will was a dullard for trying to explain such simple things.

Will reached out, tousled the boy's blond hair. "You're pretty smart, did you know that?"

"What'd I do?"

"You made me see that I don't really hate Uncle Mickey."

"Is that good?"

"Very good."

Will started the car, drove along the sun-dappled, familiar street to Elena's. The memories of good times with Mickey were thundering through him, memories he had done his best to burn. But unlike those photographs he had sent up in smoke, the memories remained. They hurt. There was no doubt of the pain. It was the pain of missing him, though, not of anger. Will knew it was a pain that could heal. He knew that no matter what Mickey had done—even murder, even that gun to Lisa's head—none of it could take away all of Will's memories, all of his love for the man who had raised him.

He turned into Elena's driveway, and Lisa came out onto the porch. Terry got out of the car, ran to her, and she wrapped him in her arms. But over her son's head, her eyes were all for Will.

His heart seemed to turn over in his chest at the sight of her. All this time, she had been trying to make him see what had been a simple truth. The things Mickey had taught him, the lessons about honor, family and loyalty, were good lessons. Mickey hadn't lived them, but Will did. Will always would. He wanted to pass those lessons on to Terry. He wanted to live his life with Lisa.

As he stared at Lisa, the negative baggage he had been carrying with him for weeks began to melt. For along with accepting that Mickey wasn't all bad, Will also realized he wasn't to blame for what the man had done. And there was no reason why he and Lisa couldn't be together. He loved her. Her life wouldn't be any better without him. If they stayed apart, both of them would have only half of what they deserved. By staying apart, they would tip the scales in favor of Mickey's dark side. And that just couldn't be.

Her gaze still locked with Will's, Lisa said to Terry, "Go inside. Elena wants to see you. You worried her, you know. We'll talk about this running-away business in a little while."

Terry went inside, calling Elena's name.

And Will and Lisa went into each other's arms.

"I've been a fool," he murmured, drawing in her sweet, special scent.

She stepped back, framed his face with her hands. "I love you, Will Espinoza. You're stubborn, idealistic to a fault, and you make me angry enough to say things I've never thought. But I love you."

"And I love you."

She lifted her lips for his kiss, then snuggled against him with a contented sigh. "We made a terrible mistake, Will. When the world got tough, we pulled apart instead of together."

"Never again."

She stepped back, looked into his eyes. "I need you, you know. It's been hard, pretending to be so strong that I didn't need you. Will, I do trust you. I've always trusted you."

"I know that."

"The last few months would have been so much easier if we had just held on to our trust in one another."

Will drew a hand through her silky hair. "From now on, partner, you can depend on me."

"You'll cover me?"

His laugh was suggestive. "In any way you want."

"Come on," she said, drawing him up the drive. "You and I are always trying to give the neighbors a show. Let's go in."

He slipped an arm around her shoulders. "I've got a million things I want to say to you. About us. About your incredibly smart son." He paused. "And about Mickey."

The healing had begun, Lisa thought, glancing at him. Joy flooded through her. Now the rest of their lives truly could begin.

Epilogue

Lisa stood back from the Christmas tree to study the results of her decorating. "What do you think?"

From her wheelchair, where she was supervising, Elena said, "It's magnificent. I've never done better myself."

The two women smiled at each other, and Lisa glanced to the top of the tree, where the cream-and-gold angel was perched. "She looks happy to be back where she belongs, don't you think?"

Elena's smile was brilliant. "Why shouldn't she be happy with a family like this to stand guard over?"

Grinning, Lisa patted the older woman on the arm. They were a wonderful family. Strong. Happy. At peace.

They had survived the tragedy of Mickey's duplicity and death, and emerged as a solid family unit. Lisa and Will were both back on the force, once again happy with their jobs. They had married in March, when the spring flowers were just beginning to bud. She had sold her home, he his condo and they had all moved into Elena's house. Together, as a family, they had faced her financial problems.

People where always asking Lisa if she minded living with Elena. But why should she mind? This house had been designed for a family. And Lisa loved Elena. She loved letting Marta cook. And now that there was a baby coming, she was happy it would come into this big, extended and loving family.

Will and Terry came crashing in the front door at that moment, laughing, trading the ridiculous jokes that Terry still loved. Her son may have shot up four inches this year, but he hadn't changed in all the fundamental ways. Terry spent plenty of time with his father. He was philosophical about the times the man let him down. Rich still wasn't perfect. But Terry had Will to fill in the empty spaces.

"You're late," Lisa told her men as they came into the living room. "Marta has dinner ready."

Will swept her into his arms, kissed her thoroughly. "Our being late just gave you more time to anticipate me."

"Yuck," Terry said, as was expected. "Come on, Elena, let's leave 'em to it." Laughing, they went out of the room.

And in the lights of the Christmas tree, under the wise gaze of the angel, Lisa and Will smiled into each other's eyes, secure in their love, happy with their family circle.

* * * * *

Silhouette

SPECIAL EDITION™

VOWS
A series celebrating marriage
by Sherryl Woods

To Love, Honor and Cherish—these were the words that three generations of Halloran men promised their women they'd live by. But these vows made in love are each challenged by the tests of time....

In October—Jason Halloran meets his match in *Love* #769;
In November—Kevin Halloran rediscovers love—with his wife—in *Honor* #775;
In December—Brandon Halloran rekindles an old flame in *Cherish* #781.

These three stirring tales are coming down the aisle toward you—only from Silhouette Special Edition!

What a year for romance!

Silhouette has five fabulous romance collections coming your way in 1993. Written by popular Silhouette authors, each story is a sensuous tale of love and life—as only Silhouette can give you!

Three bachelors are footloose and fancy-free...until now.
(March)

Heartwarming stories that celebrate the joy of motherhood.
(May)

Put some sizzle into your summer reading with three of Silhouette's hottest authors.
(June)

Take a walk on the dark side of love—with tales just perfect for those misty autumn nights.
(October)

Share in the joy of yuletide romance with four award-winning Silhouette authors.
(November)

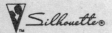

A romance for all seasons—it's always time for romance with Silhouette!